MY BEST FRIEND'S BROTHER

MAKE HER MINE SERIES-BOOK 1

ALEXIS WINTER

IT'S NO SECRET I'VE ALWAYS HAD A CRUSH ON MY BEST FRIEND'S OLDER BROTHER.

**He's the center of every single one of my naughty fantasies,
And my new boss...**

That cocky grin and those broad, athletic shoulders.
He's a walking, talking temptation.
You know what they say about a man with big hands right?

Growing up, we always tormented one another.
I was the nagging, annoying little girl he hated,
And he was the arrogant, douchebag I couldn't seem to get over.

I know he's a heartbreaker.
I know he's completely off-limits.
I KNOW my best friend would kill me.

But when I find out he wants me just as bad,
My panties melt faster than an ice cream cone in hell.
One little taste can't hurt, right?

It will stay our dirty little secret...or will it?

1

JAZMINE

"What exactly are we looking for?" my best friend, Maddie, asks as I drag her through yet, another store in the mall.

"Something that will make me look professional for my first day of work tomorrow. You know, a nice skirt with a cute top, or a dress suit. Something that will make me look like a well put-together adult but at the same time bring out all my best features." I smile, happy with my description.

Her blue eyes squint at me and her plump, pink lips narrow into a straight line. "So something sexy enough to get my brother's attention, but not so sexy that you'll be fired. Got it." She shoots me a wink as she points her long index finger at me.

I laugh off her comment and playfully smack her arm as I glide past her. "You of all people know that I don't care how your stupid brother looks at me." Just hearing myself say this sentence is laughable. Everyone knows I've had a crush on Damon since the moment I set eyes on him when I was five years old, even though I'd never in a million lifetimes admit it. In fact, I've been very adamant about denying any and all feelings for him for the better part of my life. I mean, if I never say it out loud, is it even true?

"Yeah, keep telling yourself that," Maddie says, tossing her brown hair over her shoulder as she picks up a dark gray skirt. She shows it to me with wide, excited eyes.

I scrunch my nose. "Too short." I grab another skirt off the next rack and show it to her.

"Too long." She scrunches up her nose the same way I did. "Next store?"

I purse my lips together and nod. "Guess so," I agree.

We both hang the skirts back on the racks and head out, in search of another store.

"How are you going to decorate that new office?" she asks as we walk through the mall, our heels clicking on the shiny white floor.

I laugh. "I don't even know if I'll have an office. It is your brother that got me the job after all."

She turns and looks at me with a *yeah right* face. "Exactly. He knows you've put in your time and know what you're doing. If anyone is going to root for you there, it will be him. God knows I can't do it from where I'm at."

"I just graduated, Maddie. I have to start from the bottom and work my way up. I don't have any expectations or the idea that I will be treated differently than any other new graduate."

She snorts at my statement but keeps walking.

"I'll probably end up in the copy room or pushing papers for the first year." I nod. "And I'm okay with that. I'm nothing if not determined." I flash her a quick smile.

She rolls her blue eyes. "How about this place?" she asks, pausing in front of another shop.

I shrug. "Might as well."

A little while later, we're walking out with my perfect outfit: a black pencil skirt, a light blue, button-up shirt that has bell sleeves, a wide belt, and a pair of black pumps. Maddie says the soft blue shirt makes my olive skin glow. Already I can see myself in this outfit with a pair of black framed glasses and my blonde hair pulled up into a bun. I bet I will make Damon give me second look if nothing else. Now, I'll just need to find me a fake pair of glasses to give him dirty librarian fantasies.

Thinking about Damon causes a sigh to escape my mouth. I've been in love with him for as long as I can remember, but he's never treated me like anything other than his sister's annoying friend. I understood when we were younger. I mean, he is three years older than me. No high school senior wants to be seen with a freshman. But now that we're adults and out in the real world, I thought things would change. The way he acts toward me is the same he's always acted: like an older kid picking on the smaller one. He plays tricks, calls me names, and picks on me just as much as he always has. For a while, I thought that was just his way of keeping himself in check, like he couldn't see me as a woman if he thought of me as a kid sister, but he's never shown any *real* interest, and that makes my stomach hurt. I feel like the same teenage girl that had to sit back and watch as he went out with a different girl every weekend, watching as they touched and kissed him the way I wanted to.

Without even meaning to, my head drifts back to the night I spied on him with his date from Maddie's bedroom window. Before my eyes, I can see him as he helps her out of the truck and pushes her against it before moving in for a kiss. My stomach tightens as the jealous fire burns hot inside of me. But I quickly put it out by imagining that girl being me. I can feel his soft lips against mine. I can taste his sweet flavor. I can smell his delicious cologne that always makes me a little weak in the knees.

"Seriously, stop daydreaming about my brother. It's disgusting," Maddie says, snapping me from my thoughts.

"What? I'm not thinking about Damon!" I nearly shriek.

She snorts in laughter. "Yes, you are. You always get that stupid look on your face."

"What look?" I cross my arms as we step onto the escalator.

"Your eyes start to shine, then glaze over. Your lips turn up just a bit at the corners, and your cheeks turn pink. You start breathing faster, like just picturing him gets your heart racing," she says all breathy and dramatic.

"No, it doesn't," I argue, even though, he truly does make my heart race and has for many years.

Damon has always been the athletic type. In high school, he played every sport our school had to offer. Baseball, basketball, football, track, and wrestling. In college, he stuck with basketball and track, but damn how I missed seeing him in that wrestling uniform.

His skin is tanned year-round from spending as much time as he can outside, and his muscles are firm and toned from so much activity. His dark brown hair is almost always styled, but the way it looks all messy after a run is sexy as fuck too. And his green eyes, with just a hint of blue, they cut right through me every time he looks my way.

"Ugh, stop! You're doing it again."

I laugh and bump my shoulder against hers. "Shut up." I glance down at the bottom level and my eyes land on the pretzel stand. "Have time for a cinnamon-sugar pretzel?"

She smiles wide. "Of course."

We giggle as we run from the escalator to the stand.

"This time, it's on me. I feel like you're going to need as much sugar as you can stand to put up with my brother eight hours a day," she says before ordering and handing over her card.

"He's not that bad, Maddie."

"Yeah, but sometimes he's a total douche-canoe."

We both laugh as we take our sugar pretzel to a nearby table.

MY ALARM GOES off at six and I pop up, excited to get to my first day of work. I'm still tired since I had trouble falling asleep last night because I'm so nervous, but the excitement pumping through my body energizes me enough to keep going, to move faster.

After turning off the alarm, I nearly run to the bathroom to shower. An hour later, I stand back and look myself over in the mirror. My new outfit looks amazing. The pencil skirt hugs my hips and has a slit up the back, giving just a peek of my tanned legs, which now have a nice shape thanks to the black pumps. The baby blue top flatters my thin frame and shows just a touch of cleavage—not enough to think I'm looking for attention, but enough to show off my womanly curves. I pulled my hair up into a neat bun and added just a little makeup: some shimmery eyeshadow, a little brown eyeliner and mascara, and a layer of peach lipstick.

Happy with my appearance, I grab my purse and keys and head out. Living in Chicago, I opt to hail a cab instead of trying to walk the six blocks in these heels. Most of the time, I walk where I need to be. If it's too far, I stick with the bus, but today, I want to be early. I don't want to take the chance of having a baby spit up on me or someone spill their coffee down my top. Today, I want the quiet time to prepare myself. Hopefully, this is the first day of the rest of my life. I laugh at how stupid that sounds, but seriously. This is the job I've worked years for. If I can get it, I'm never letting it go.

The cab comes to a stop in front of a tall glass building. The sign on the front reads: Windsor Wealth Management. It causes a surge of excitement and happiness to bubble deep within my stomach. Without saying a word, I hand over the cash and step out, still gawking at the big fancy building.

I take a deep breath and snap myself out of the trance I'm stuck in. "It's okay, Jazz. You can do this. Just go in there and show 'em what you've got," I tell myself, needing a pep talk.

As I walk across the concrete, I dig around in my purse for the piece of paper I was mailed; reading over it, I find the directions for my first time in the building: *First thing, please go to room 107—Internal Affairs—to receive your work I.D. and to fill out your tax information.*

The revolving door spins, and I jump inside, feeling like a hamster in a wheel until I step into the building, my steps echoing against the granite floor. There's a big sign in the foyer, one side is a list of names while the other side has room numbers and floor level. I find that room 107 is located on the ground floor, and I quickly walk up to the receptionist.

"Windsor Wealth Management, please hold," she says, pushing buttons on the phone. "Can I help you?" she asks, giving me her attention.

"Room 107?" I ask, motioning toward the hallway on her right and the one of her left.

She smiles sweetly. "To your left." She clicks another button. "Windsor Wealth Management, please hold."

"Thank you," I whisper, not trying to disturb her as I head to my left.

After I've filled out all the employment forms and had my picture taken for my employee I.D., I read the next step on my paper: *Please go to the fifth floor and see the receptionist.*

I walk back into the lobby and over to the elevators. There's already a small group of people waiting to get on. I join them and continue reading over my instructions as I wait.

"Look at what we have here," I hear someone say, looking up just in time to see Damon coming to a stop beside me. My heart momentarily halts in my chest at the sight of him. He's dressed in a well-pressed black suit with a white shirt and red tie. His dark hair is styled neatly, and he's wearing a grin on his lips, his green eyes sparkling with mischief.

Even though I want to fall at his feet and ask how I can please him, I reign myself back in, crossing my arms over my chest and narrowing my eyes at him. "Ugh, I wasn't expecting to see you so early in the morning. I can tell I'm going to need a lot more coffee."

He laughs, clearly having fun with me already. He loves getting under my skin, and I think he loves it even more when I give him shit right back. His eyes quickly glance down my body and back to my eyes. "You clean up much better than I pictured. I mean, look at you." He motions toward me. "I was half expecting cut-off jean shorts, a flannel, and biker boots." He winks at me, knowing damn well I would never dress like that for work.

"That was one Halloween, and I'll never live it down." I shake my head while holding off my smile. I remember that Halloween very well.

"What do you think, Maddie?" I ask, stepping out of my bathroom and into the bedroom where she's waiting on me.

She looks me up and down, her mouth hanging open and her eyes wide. "You look freaking amazing, Jazz! I mean, you could get into a night club like this!" She's walking circles around me.

I smile, happy with her praises, as I turn and study my reflection in the mirror. I'm supposed to be a punk rocker, and I guess I do look punk rock, but the only reason I picked this was to show some skin to get Damon's attention. My blonde hair has streaks of hot pink, blue, and purple—temporary, of course—my eye makeup is thick and black as night. I have a fake nose ring in, and my lips are painted a deep, dark red. I'm wearing a black tube top, showing off my firm stomach, but keeping a tad classy by putting on the red and black flannel I leave hanging open. I'm wearing the shortest pair of cut-off jean shorts I could find, paired with ripped fishnets and biker boots.

"Let's go to my house so I can get ready," she says, grabbing my hand and pulling me along behind her. I let out a sigh of relief when we make it through the house without my mom seeing this crazy outfit. No way would she let me out of the house like this.

Just as we're walking up the drive at Maddie's house, Damon is stepping out of his brand-new truck.

"Sup, dork?" Maddie says, walking past him.

He opens his mouth to say something back, but his words fall short as I walk into his view. His eyes are wide, and his mouth is hanging open just like Maddie's was, but he's fighting off a smile.

"What are you supposed to be?" he asks, walking a circle around me. I turn my head to watch him. His eyes are moving up and down my body, and my thighs tighten as my cheeks burn.

"A punk-rocker. Duh," I say, hoping he didn't notice the way my voice was cutting out.

He comes to a stop in front of me, but now, he's not amused: he's concerned. "Your mom let you out like that?" He motions toward me.

I roll my eyes. "What's it to you?"

"Where you two going tonight?" he asks, glancing between Maddie and me.

"Why?" Maddie asks, stepping up to my side.

"With her dressed like that," he points at me, "you're going to need someone to get you out of the trouble you're going to be in. I'm coming to whatever party you're going to."

Inside, I smile, but outwardly, I groan, just like Maddie.

Just thinking about the way he was looking at me that night makes my temperature rise.

I turn to look at him and notice he's looking at me like that right now. He's holding back a grin, eyes glistening and moving around quickly like he's trying not to look at me.

"What?" I ask, no longer able to hold back my grin.

"Huh?" He acts like he didn't hear me.

"Why are you looking at me like that?" I turn my body to face him directly.

"Like what?" He frowns.

I laugh and shake my head as I turn back to face the elevators. "Keep your eyes to yourself before I alert HR."

This makes him bust out laughing. "Don't flatter yourself, Jazz. I'm still amazed you made it to work on time."

2

DAMON

Seeing her at that elevator makes me do a double take. This isn't the little Jazmine I grew up with. She isn't the knobby-kneed kid that always ate the last slice of pizza. She isn't the pesky teenage girl that spied on me with my dates. Hell, this isn't even the girl I saw just two weeks ago that was lounging on my sister's couch in cat-print pajamas and eating ice cream straight out of the carton while mocking me. This is a whole new Jazmine—a grown woman with breasts I want to see, curves I want to memorize, and mile-long legs that I want to run my hand up.

I shake my head and rub my eyes, needing to get her out of my mind to focus on work

A ding fills my ears and the doors open, allowing us all to step inside. I'm standing in the back, and she's right in front of me in the crowded elevator. It gives me the perfect chance to check out her ass without her seeing me. I let my eyes fall slightly. They nearly bug out of my head when I see how round and plump her ass looks under that tight pencil skirt. It's slit up the back—not high, just to her lower thigh—but her toned calves and those shoes make me want to see more. Already, I'm picturing how they'd look wrapped around my hips.

What the fuck am I doing? This isn't just some random woman that walked into the elevator. This is Jazzy. The little girl that always said my breath smelled like farts, and that any girl that kissed me must like pink eye because coming that close to an asshole was sure to give it to them. Just thinking of that makes me laugh. She was always so damn mouthy and quick-witted.

The sound of me laughing in the quiet elevator makes everyone turn around and look at me, even Jazz. She frowns, looks me up and down to make sure I'm not taping a *kick me* sign to her back, then turns back around.

Fuck my life. My job just got ten times harder. Why did I get her this job? I must be glutton for punishment.

When the doors open, she walks out, and I'm right behind her. She hasn't realized that I'm following because I haven't told her about this part of the job yet. She stops at the reception desk and I stay behind so she won't see me.

"Hi, I'm Jazmine Hernandez. This is my first day, and I was told to come to you."

Lisa, the receptionist, smiles, her eyes flashing from Jazz to me and back. "It's nice to meet you, Ms. Hernandez." She stands and holds out her hand to shake. "I guess you haven't been told yet, but Mr. Strickland will be overseeing your work. So you just need to follow him." She motions toward me.

Jazz turns around with a look of surprise painted on her face. Her mouth is open, and her brown eyes are wide, until she sees me, that is. When her eyes land on mine, her mouth snaps shut and her eyes narrow, causing a small wrinkle to form between them.

I walk closer with my smile in place. I point at her. "Keep that up and you'll have wrinkles for sure. Follow me." I immediately turn and walk to my closed office door.

"I have a feeling I'm going to need Botox after today," she mumbles, causing me to laugh under my breath.

I open my office door and hold it open until she comes in. Closing the door behind us, I take a seat behind my desk while she stands in the center of the room, looking at the desks on either end.

"So, why didn't you tell me you'd be overseeing my work?" she asks, walking toward the floor to ceiling windows and looking out at the busy city below.

I shrug. "I figured you wouldn't take the job if I told you what it was."

She turns to face me slowly with a look of horror on her face. "What is the job, exactly?"

"My assistant." I kick my feet up, getting comfortable.

Her shoulders visibly fall, and her eyes close while a long breath escapes her beautiful, plump lips. "You have to be joking." She slowly walks over to my desk and has a seat on the opposite side.

"I'm not but hear me out." I sit up, placing my elbows on the top of the desk as I lean closer to her. "Getting your foot in the door is the hard part, right?"

She nods her head, silently agreeing with me.

"Well, see there! Hard part over." I grin, proud of myself. "Now, all we have to do is slowly bring you into meetings where you can put your two cents in, and sooner rather than later, hopefully, you'll be hired on in whatever department you want. You'll just have to put up with me for a couple months to do it. And," I add on, holding up my finger to silence her, "it'll be a whole lot faster than standing out there interviewing with those fifty other graduates all trying to get the job you want."

She groans and rolls her head back, so she's staring up at the ceiling. "Fine." She stands and starts pacing the floor with her hands on her hips. "This will just be like the time I lost that bet and had to be your slave for the week. I can do that." She's sticking out her lip while nodding her head. She's clearly trying to talk herself into staying. "I mean, it's what? Fetching coffee, making copies, answering phones, and taking messages? That sort of thing, right?" She stops her pacing and looks at me for confirmation.

I nod. "Pretty much... and you know, chasing out crazy women that've slept with me but refuse to leave." I grin, causing her to give me her angry eyes.

I laugh. "I'm just joking. Everything will be professional. I promise."

She takes a deep breath while nodding once, letting her arms fall to her sides. "Okay. Where do we start?"

I smile. "I'm glad you asked." I stand and pick up a file folder off my desk. "I have a meeting this morning and need thirty copies of every page in this file to hand out." I pass it over to her.

She presses her lips into a straight line but takes it. "And the copy room is where?"

"End of the hall," I reply, taking my seat once again and turning my attention to the computer screen to check this morning's emails.

Without a word, she turns for the door, and my eyes jump up to watch her go. With her every step, her hips sway from side to side, and I get just a peek at her shapely legs. She stops when she gets to the door and turns back to me. "You're doing it again," she says around a smile.

My eyes jump from her ass to her eyes. "Doing what?"

"Looking at me." Her dark eyes roll.

"For the last time, I'm not looking at you. Do you need a cereal box to put between us like when we were kids?" I ask, amused but also using a deeper tone of voice to make her think I'm getting annoyed by her.

She points a manicured finger at me. "That's not a bad idea," she says, walking out and closing the door behind her.

I sit back in my chair, and my eyes land on her desk right across the room from mine. If I sit here and she sits there, and we both look up, we'll be eye to eye. I can't handle that. Then an idea hits me. Way back in grade school, when we'd take tests, we used two folders and stand them up on the edges of our desk so you couldn't see your neighbor's paper. No way can I have all that shit cluttering my desk.

I open my bottom desk drawer and pull out a stack of unused file folders. I stand with the stack in hand and walk over to her desk, placing each one up so when she sits down, all she'll see is folders instead of me. This will also help me keep my eyes to myself. I've been caught checking her out enough already.

When I'm proud of my handy work, I turn my attention back to the computer screen and go through all the unread emails. I spend a good thirty minutes sorting through them all, replying when necessary, and deleting what's not needed. I look up and find that Jazz still isn't back. I decide to look for her to make sure she hasn't gotten lost.

I exit the office and walk back toward the elevators, down the hall, and into the copy room. I find Jazz leaning against the copy machine, holding a big stack of papers and smiling while James flirts with her.

Walking into the room steals both their attention, and the conversation stops.

I slide my hands into my pockets and smile while glancing between them. "I was worried you got lost," I say, finally keeping my eyes on her.

She smiles. "I'm sorry, I was just finishing up when James walked in. We got carried away talking."

He forces his smile to fall. "I'm sorry. I didn't mean to hold you up. I just noticed that small tattoo on her ankle," he says, now looking at me. "And I knew I had to talk to her. Blink-182 is my favorite band."

With his words, I look at her ankle and see a small tattoo of a smiley face that has X's for eyes and arrows coming out the side. How have I never noticed this before? When did she get a tattoo? Does she have more? If so, where are they? My mind starts to drift, but I catch myself quickly, turning back to the conversation at hand.

I nod once. "Not a problem," I reply, bringing my attention to her face. "We need to get some more work done before my meeting."

She smiles and nods. "I'll be right there."

I turn and leave, but not before giving James one last look, a silent warning, if you will: *Don't fuck with her. She's mine.*

On my walk back to the office, I think about those words: She's mine. Where the fuck did that even come from? I guess in a way she's always been mine. Mine to torture. Mine to tease. Mine to protect. She's no different than my sister. Just thinking that makes me want to gag. Okay, she's different than my sister.

Fuck, I don't even know what I'm thinking, or feeling for that matter. All I know is I don't want her with James. James is a player. Once he gets what he wants, she'll be heartbroken.

Just as I'm sitting down at my desk, she walks in. Her eyes land on her desk before meeting mine.

"Really?" She motions toward my handy work.

I shrug. "I didn't have cereal boxes. Next best thing?" I ask with a raise of my brow and a smirk.

She rolls her eyes and walks over to me, placing the stack of papers on my desk.

"I need those stapled together in order, please."

"Seriously? There's like four-hundred pages there. You could have told me beforehand so I could have had the machine do it." Her brows are arched high.

I nod. "Why do you think I came looking for you? We're running out of time. There's a stapler in your desk." I motion across the room.

She picks up the stack of papers and walks to her desk, grumbling something under her breath.

I watch her go until she sits down and she's no longer in my view. I smile to myself. This was a better idea than I thought.

I sit upright and bring up the notepad app on my computer to make a note on topics to cover at today's meeting. I place my fingers on the keyboard to start but the sound of very loud stapling cuts through the silence.

BAM. A folder on her desk topples over and falls.

I stop before I can even start on my document and look over at her desk.

BAM. Another folder topples and falls.

It sounds like she's punching the stapler.

BAM.

"Seriously, what the hell are you doing over there?"

She slowly stands, her head moving upward into view. "Stapling these papers like you asked."

"Are you in a fight with the stapler? I've never in my life heard such aggressive stapling."

She smiles sweetly. "Just doing my job." She shrugs one shoulder before lowering herself back into her seat, out of my view.

BAM.

I let out a deep breath and hang my head, trying to clear my anger and annoyance.

BAM. The sound of ruffling papers fills the room.

BAM.

BAM.

BAM.

"Enough!" I yell, standing up so quickly my chair rolls back and bumps into the filing cabinets.

The sound stops.

I walk around her desk. I pick up the small group of papers and place them in the stapler. Easily, I press down and staple them together with only the slightest hint of a noise. "See? That's how you do it." I look down at her smiling face.

"Ohhhh, I see." She takes the next stack and slides them into the stapler. Gently, she presses down just as I've shown her. And, no noise.

"Much better," I say, walking back to my desk.

The moment I sit down,

BAM.

I throw myself back in my seat as I close my eyes and talk myself out of killing her.

3

JAZMINE

I snicker to myself, knowing I'm driving him crazy. But what does he expect? I mean, he basically tricked me into this job. I understand his reasoning: it will be easier to get the job I want if I'm already a part of the company. But he could've told me that when he offered to put in a good word for me. Instead, he let me walk into another one of his jokes. You'd think by now I'd be used to his tricks. I should have foreseen this.

Regardless, I'm in the company, I have a paying job, I get to look at his handsome face all day, and I get to drive him crazy. I guess there are worse jobs I could've gotten. Plus, James is pretty cute, and I never would've met him without this job. And, I might be crazy, but I saw a hint of jealousy on Damon's face when he walked in and found us talking.

I continue to staple the papers as loudly as possible while letting my mind drift off. Damon doesn't say another word; he knows what I'm doing, and he's choosing to ignore it because, really, he can't do anything about it anyway. And maybe the more I annoy him, the faster he'll work at getting me out of his office and into one of my own. I would never try this tactic had my boss been anyone but Damon.

A knock at the door pulls me from my thoughts, and I peek up over my folders to find Damon looking at me. His eyes are wide, and his brows are lifted.

"Oh, I answer the door?" I ask, standing up and rushing to it. Pulling it open, a woman with dark hair walks in without acknowledging me.

"There you are," she says, walking directly over to Damon's desk.

I see him let out a long breath before forcing a smile onto his face. Whoever she is, he's not happy to see her.

"Here I am," he replies, using his fake happy tone. He stands, and she rushes to him, pulling him in for a hug.

"I've been searching for you all morning. I wanted to talk to you about tonight's gala." She pulls away but keeps her hands on his biceps.

I shut the door, and the noise causes them both to look at me.

Taking the hint I've been smacked with, I turn and take my seat at my desk, out of their view thanks to the folders Damon so sweetly decided to put up.

"About that," I hear him say softly.

"Oh, no. Don't tell me you're pulling out early." I can hear the smile on her face. It makes her voice take on a flirty tone.

I roll my eyes.

Damon lets out a nervous laugh. "I'm sorry. Something has come up, and I won't be able to make it. You know I would if I could."

She lets out a deep breath that even I can hear from clear across the room. "I know you would. You never turn down a night out with me. Mostly because a night out turns into a night in." Her voice gets a tad louder, like she's turning and facing me now. Is she trying to make me jealous?

I hear him let out a soft laugh and finally, my curiosity gets the best of me, and I peek out over the top of the folders in time to see her turn her head back in his direction.

Her hands are holding onto his neck, and his hands are on her hips. Their embrace makes acid burn in my throat.

"I'm sorry, Abby," he says softly.

"I understand... this time. But you better not stand me up again. I won't wait around for you forever, you know."

She releases him but catches his hand in hers and pulls him over to the door.

"What can I say? A woman like you must have plenty of back-ups waiting to take my place." He gives her a flirty smile.

She laughs and then pulls him in for a long, noisy, wet-sounding kiss.

My eyes grow in size as my face wrinkles in disgust.

Finally, she pulls away, and he opens the door, closing it the moment she steps out.

When he turns back around, I see him quickly wipe at his mouth, and I jump back into my stapling.

"Okay, out with it," he says, walking closer to me so I can see his red face above my folders.

"What?" I ask, quickly pulling my lips between my teeth and biting down on them to keep the smile away.

"I know you have something to say. You always do."

"Nope." I shake my head.

He moves a couple of the folders and sits on the edge of my desk, looking down at me. "Really? You, Miss Queen of Wit, have nothing to say?"

My smile begins to break free. "Nothing at all."

He shrugs and stands, walking back to his side of the room. I turn my attention back to my papers, but he spins around.

"I'm not seeing her if that's what you're thinking."

"I wasn't thinking that at all," I say, not looking anywhere but at my papers. But his words do take that sour taste from my mouth.

"She was a business deal."

This gets my attention. My eyes pop up to meet his.

"There was this thing." He shakes his head. "Anyway, I had to take her out to keep her attention away from certain things. It worked, but now I can't get her to leave me alone."

"Good to know." I nod once and turn back to my work.

"Good to know?"

I nod again, not speaking.

Damon shakes his head, turns around, and takes his seat, letting the conversation drop.

When lunch rolls around, I make my way outside, where I bump into Maddie.

"How's the first day going?" she asks, rushing to my side.

I frown at her. "I should've eaten more of that pretzel yesterday."

She giggles and puts her arm around my shoulders, pulling me toward the sidewalk so we can grab some lunch.

"See? Total douche-canoe."

I nod in agreement.

"So, did you meet any new guys?" Maddie asks as we share a plate of wings.

I pick up my beer and wash down my last bite. "There was this one guy I met in the copy room. He noticed my tattoo."

Her blue eyes grow wide. "What's his name? What's he look like? Is he hot? Did he ask you out?"

"Whoa, slow down." I hold up my hand, palm facing her. "His name is James. He's tall and thin. He has dirty-blond hair and blue eyes. He's cute, but not hot. And no, he didn't ask me out. I think he was going to, but then your stupid brother walked in and scared him off."

She scoffs. "Story of my life, sista."

"You know what's crazy though?"

"What's that?" she asks, eyes popping up to meet mine.

"I could have sworn that..." I shake my head. "Never mind."

"What? Tell me," she demands.

"Well, it's just that I've caught Damon checking me out several times today."

She laughs. "It's probably your ass in that tight skirt, or your boobs spilling over that shirt. I mean, you look hot, Jazz."

"So, you don't think it means anything?" I ask quietly.

Her facial expression softens. "I don't think so, honey. It's not you. It's just my brother. He's a complete dumbass and he's totally driven by his dick. I mean, I've caught him checking out old ladies in yoga pants."

I laugh. "What is it with guys and yoga pants?"

She shrugs. "Just don't get your hopes up."

"I won't," I agree, going back to our wings and beer.

"Why don't you download one of those dating apps?" Maddie asks while wiping her fingers free of hot sauce.

I scoff. "Seriously? I'm not trying to get murdered."

She giggles and shakes her head. "I'm not talking about a hook-up site. I'm talking about an actual dating site, where you can talk to the person a while before actually meeting them in a very public place." She put emphasis on the word *public*.

I shrug one shoulder and check my watch. "I'll think about it, but I have to go before your stupid brother gives me another ridiculous job to do." I drop a twenty on the table, throw my purse over my shoulder, and stand, giving her a quick hug before running off.

I'm walking back into the office with less than a minute to spare.

"Pushing it close, aren't you?" Damon teases with a grin on his sexy lips.

I hold up my middle finger as I bend down and pick up all of the fallen folders. I take a seat at my desk and lock my eyes on his as I put every single folder back in place so we can't see one another. All I can hear is his deep chuckle.

"I was just joking with that, you know?"

I know, but I will get more work done if I can't see your gorgeous face, I think.

"Hey, a good idea is a good idea," I tell him.

The next thing I know, he's standing over my desk, removing the folders. He perches on the edge and looks down at me with a grin.

"What?" I ask.

"You're cute when you're angry."

My mouth starts to drop open from being speechless. That's the first time he's ever said I was cute.

Someone knocks on the door and enters quickly. "Damon, Bennett wants to see you," a lady says.

Damon looks down at me, smile still in place. "Be right back," he says as he stands and walks out of the office.

When I'm alone, a breath I didn't realize I was holding escapes. Did he really say I was cute? Did he mean it? Did he mean it as I'm cute cute, or I'm little-sister cute? My heart starts racing, and butterflies fill my stomach. But then I remember Maddie's warning and my stomach sinks.

Maybe Maddie is right. Maybe I should join a dating app. At least, if nothing else, it will help keep my mind off Damon. And hey, I may even fall in love. I pull out my phone and search until I find one that doesn't look completely cheesy. It only takes a second to put in all my information and snap a quick picture of myself for my profile. Since I don't have any real work to do until I'm assigned a new job, I put all my attention on my phone while filling out all the questions.

Idea of the perfect date: A quick dinner from whatever stand is nearby, lots of beer, and an action-packed show (monster trucks, dirt bikes, bull riding).

Favorite eye color: Green with a hint of blue.

Favorite hair color: Dark chocolate.

Idea of the perfect mate: Tall, lean, but with muscles to run my hands over. Must have a good sense of humor and be able to take a joke. Work-oriented, but also able to leave work at the door and enjoy his time away.

Without even realizing it, every answer screams Damon.

I let out a deep breath and roll my eyes. I'm doomed.

The door opens, and I nearly jump out of my skin. Damon smiles as he closes the door and walks over to me. "Whatcha doing? Looking at porn?" he laughs.

"No! Why in the world would you think that?" I frown at him in disgust.

He shrugs as he glances down at my phone. "In my experience, when someone jumps that high with their phone in their hand, they're watching porn." He turns and walks back to his desk.

I turn my phone off and place it inside my purse so I can fulfill the next task I'm given.

———————

WHEN THE DAY FINALLY ENDS, I practically rush from the office. I'm feeling a little let down because I was really looking forward to starting this job, and it's not exactly as I imagined it. But at the same time, I'm also happy that I've gotten to spend eight whole hours with Damon. I'm not sure if that's a good thing or a bad thing. Normally, I would say a good thing, but now, I'm afraid that spending this much time with him will only make the feelings I have for him that much stronger. And since he doesn't seem to have any serious interest in me, that could end up hurting me.

I'm so confused that I don't want to do anything but strip off my clothes and sink into a tub of hot, bubbly water. Which is exactly what I do the moment I step inside my apartment. With the bubbles covering my entire body, I reach down and pick up my phone off the table beside the big, white, claw-foot tub. I turn it back on for the first time since leaving work, and the dating app I downloaded has ten notifications. I smile to myself, just thinking about having that many men wanting to date me.

The notifications all say *so-and-so wants to become friends*. It also shows a small picture. I scroll through until I find a picture that catches my eye. He has dark brown hair, a sexy smile that shows his perfectly straight, white teeth, and blue eyes. I click on the notification, and it takes me to his page. His name is Brandon Harris. I accept his friend request and hit the home button. I'm preparing to turn off the screen and put it down to sink deeper into the tub, but an alert goes off, and the notification reads: *Private message from Brandon Harris*. A smile forms on its own as I swipe the screen and bring up the message.

4

DAMON

When I leave work, I go straight home. I walk in the front door and to the fridge to grab a nice, cold beer. I pop the top and take a long drink before shrugging out of my jacket and loosening my tie. I pick the beer back up and head to the living room, where I sit in my favorite brown leather recliner. Kicking my shoes off, I unlock my phone and immediately start looking for the app that I saw Jazz using earlier.

While it downloads, I pull off my tie and belt and throw them onto the couch next to me. I turn on the TV for some background noise and take another drink. I sit watching my phone until the app is downloaded and installed. The second it becomes available, I open it and start creating a profile, since that's the only way I can view Jazz's page. I make up a fake name, something at least a thousand people on the planet have, and fill in all the questions. Finally, it asks for a photo.

Fuck.

I could add one of myself, but I don't want anyone thinking I need a dating app to find women. I could use one of my friends, but I would hate for them to stumble upon it. So, I figure my only option is to go to a stock website and purchase a photo. I scroll through hundreds of pictures of men before I find the perfect one. He even resembles me a little. He has dark hair, blue eyes, tanned skin, and he's wearing a big smile and a white dress shirt. I pay for the image and upload it to the app.

Finally, I'm in. I can search for women in my city, and it doesn't take long to find Jazz. I study her picture, noticing she took this picture at work. She wears that baby blue top, and I can see just a delicious and tempting amount of cleavage. In the background is my empty desk. I laugh to myself and click on her picture.

Would you like to send Jazmine Hernandez a friend request?

I click *yes* and start typing out a message.

'Hey, sexy,' I start, thinking maybe I'll teach her a quick lesson on using this type of app, but then an idea pops into my head.

I know Jazz has always been attracted to me, but I also think that because I'm her best friend's brother, I'd never have a chance. That and I've tormented her for her entire life. She probably hates me. Or, at least, loves me until I open my mouth. Maybe this is the only way to make her see that she doesn't hate me entirely.

I delete what I wrote and instead send, *Hello, I came across your profile and knew I had to know you. Do you have some time to chat?*

I sit, watching the screen. Little bubbles form, letting me know she's replying. A moment later, she sends back, *I have a few minutes. What do you want to talk about?*

Brandon: *I find it hard to believe you have trouble getting dates. Do you work a lot?*

Jazz: *Not really. I just don't get out much. But I guess I could say the same to you. You don't exactly have a serial killer's face.*

That makes me laugh.

Brandon: *What exactly does a serial killer face look like?*

Jazz: *Oh, you know... wide, crazy eyes, a creepy smile, holding a cat in your picture. That kind of thing.*

Brandon: *Well, my cat wasn't available the day I took the picture.* I joke.

Jazz: *LOL*

Brandon: *I'm just joking. I don't have a cat. Not that I am against them. Just don't have time.*

Jazz: *Don't have time? Do you work a lot?*

Brandon: *I have a full-time job, but when I'm not working, I don't exactly like sitting at home. I much prefer going for a run, working out, or finding someplace to go.*

Jazz: *Busybody, huh?*

Brandon: *Things in motion stay in motion... or that's what I'm told, anyway.*

Jazz: *So, where do you work?*

Brandon: *Whoa, how do I know you're not a serial killer?* I laugh just from picturing her face.

Jazz: *Well, do I have a serial killer face?*

I pick up my beer and finish it off, wondering how I should answer that.

Brandon: *No, I don't think so, at least. But I haven't met a lot of serial killers either.*

Jazz: *That you know of ;)*

Brandon: *You got me there. So, switching off the topic of serial killers, what do you like to do in your spare time?*

Jazz: *All kinds of things. Movies and dinner. I love going to any live show. Motocross, monster trucks, concerts. I have to admit; I probably spend more money on entertainment than paying bills. I like to keep things simple. I don't even have internet or cable at my place.*

Brandon: *I don't either!* I agree. *That's strange nowadays. Everybody has satellite TV and unlimited internet access. But I'd rather be out enjoying the world than sitting at home and watching it.*

Jazz: *OMG, me too! I didn't think I'd find another person like me. All my friends think I'm crazy!*

Brandon: *Me too. I never hear the end of it from my sister. She's one of those people that almost always have their phone in front of their face. She's up to date on all the YouTube scandals and Facebook drama. It's funny when she tries talking to me about that stuff. I never have any idea who she's talking about.*

Jazz: *My best friend is the same way! I can't believe we have so much in common.*

That is pretty amazing. Who knew we'd be so perfect for each other? I know that she was an annoying kid that grew into a beautiful, sexy woman, but I didn't realize we were into the same things.

Brandon: *Maybe this dating app wasn't such a bad idea at all. I admit, I was reluctant to try it out, but a friend talked me into it.*

Jazz: *Same! My friend Maddie suggested I join after watching me pine for a certain man my whole life.*

My eyes grow in size. What man is she talking about? It has to be someone she went to school with.

Brandon: *There's a girl I know, and I've recently found myself having feelings for her. But it's something that will never happen. I'm pretty sure she hates me.*

Jazz: *Why would she hate you? You seem like a pretty nice guy to me.*

Brandon: *We grew up together. And I haven't always been as charming as I am now (j/k).*

Jazz: *LOL It's so funny. Just from talking to you for these last couple minutes, I feel like I know you. I can relate to everything you're saying.*

That tells me that I need to get off here before I accidentally reveal who I really am, or before she puts two and two together and figures it out herself.

Brandon: *I really wish I could talk more, but I just got off work and need to get a few things done. Same time tomorrow?*

Jazz: *Deal. Talk to you tomorrow.*

I close out of the app and set my phone down. A long breath leaves my lips in a hurry; at the same time, my heart skips a beat. I start thinking about our conversation and wonder what guy she could've been talking about. I think back on the past when she and Maddie would talk, but I don't ever remember hearing them mention a guy's name. But, I'm sure it's not something they would talk about in front of me either. That would've only given me more ammo to fire.

For the first time in my life, I have regrets. I regret picking on her so much. I regret not making an effort to get to know her sooner: the real her. I regret marching all those girls in front of her. Maybe if I hadn't done those things, she wouldn't hate me as much as she does today. Maybe she'd even have feelings for me.

It's at this moment that I decide I'm going to make Jazmine Hernandez fall for me. I'm going to let her see the real me, not her tormentor. I no longer want to be her best friend's brother. Now, I want her, and I want her to want me.

———

I WAKE a little early in the morning and take a hot shower. I dress in my favorite suit, style my hair, and add a splash of cologne. I grab my briefcase and walk out the door. I climb behind the wheel of my Jeep Wrangler and head toward the office.

I used to get laughs showing up to work in this. I mean, you wouldn't expect to find a man dressed in a suit behind the wheel of a blacked-out Wrangler, but it's the only vehicle I will drive. I'm a businessman, but I'm a man first. I like taking my Jeep off-road. I like camping. I like driving with the top off and having the wind in my hair. I'm nothing like what people would expect of me. I'm not spending a year's salary on some fancy sports car. I don't want my car to be worth more than my house. I have a decent, normal sized house. Nothing like what the rest of the guys at work own. They all want things, material objects to make the world think they mean something. I'm nothing like that. I want experiences, not things. And I have nothing to prove to the world. I would rather use my money on vacations and adventures. I want to travel the world and do things that most people can only dream about. I think that's something that Jazz and I can agree on. She doesn't strike me as the material type. I'm sure that if I could just get her to forget our past, she'd fall in love with me and we'd be perfect together.

I park in my usual parking spot and head inside the building. I'm greeted by everyone I pass. I give them a quick hello and go straight to my office. Opening the door, I find Jazz sitting behind her desk.

"Good morning," I say, coming to a stop. "I didn't expect you here so early." I can't stop myself from looking up and down her body as she stands to bring me a cup of coffee. Her knee-length skirt hugs her hips.

She smiles as she hands over my coffee. "I slept good last night and woke up early. Figured, why not show up early and get some work done."

I take the cup and go to set down my briefcase at my desk. "Did you have a good evening last night?" I ask, slipping out of my jacket.

"It was pretty uneventful. You?" she asks, not looking up from the stack of papers on her desk.

"I didn't do much. Went home, had dinner alone, and went to sleep early."

She looks up at me with a smirk. "Couldn't find anyone to replace gala lady?"

I snort and roll my eyes. "I didn't try. I was just happy to be rid of her."

"Does she think you two are together?" she asks, a little frown marring her face.

I sit down and turn my computer on. "I have no idea what she thinks, but I've never led her to believe that." I look up to see her eyes narrow.

"What?" I ask.

"You took her out, slept with her, and kissed her yesterday. You didn't give her reason to think that?" One eyebrow arches high.

"It's not like that. I took her out as a friend. We had too much to drink and slept together. And I didn't kiss her yesterday. She kissed me," I say, pointing my finger.

"But you didn't stop that kiss either, now did you?" Now she's back to enjoying seeing me squirm.

"What are you suggesting?"

She shrugs her shoulders. "I'm suggesting that you tell her how you feel. Whether she likes it or not, it can't be wrong. I'm sure she will admire your honesty."

My heart starts beating faster. "Would you admire my honesty?"

She smiles slightly. "I would," she says with a nod.

I bite the inside of my cheek to keep myself from telling her about these new feelings I'm having. Before anything else can be said, my phone is ringing. I lean forward and answer it.

"Damon Strickland."

"Hey, man. I need you to come up to my office really quick," Bennet says.

"Be right there," I tell him, hanging up the phone. I stand and make my way toward the door. "I'll be right back. Bennet needs me up in his office," I tell Jazz.

She nods once but doesn't say anything.

I get in the elevator and hit the top floor. Bennet is the CEO of Windsor Wealth Management. We've known one another for years. We went to college together, and I think had we not been together, neither of us would be living the life we are. He helped me just as much as I helped him. And when we graduated, and his father left the business to him, I was the first person he hired. To say we're close is an understatement.

"Hello, Gladys," I say, walking past his assistant and letting myself into his office.

Bennet is standing at his drink cart, pouring two drinks when I walk in.

"What's up, man?" I ask.

He turns to face me, holding out a glass. "I'm going to be needing some help this afternoon. I have a high-profile client coming in, and I need help explaining how we lost a small portion of his retirement."

Already, my nerves skyrocket. "How much is a small portion?"

He moves his head from side to side. "A quarter of a million dollars," he replies, eyes growing wide.

"Fuck, man," I mumble under my breath as I raise the glass to my lips.

"We also have to explain how things are about to take a turn for the better, so he doesn't pull out on us completely. I mean, this man has been with us since my father started it up back in the eighties. We have to keep him happy or..." He shakes his head. "I'm afraid of what he could do." He sits down across from me. "Dad's been itching to come back, using every little excuse to get away from my mom and back into this building."

I laugh. "I knew retirement didn't suit your father."

"It was the number one reason why I was so iffy on even working here. I knew once he got bored with traveling the world, he'd want to come back, even though he assured me he wouldn't. But every time I go over there for dinner, it's just one question after another. Are you doing this, are you doing that? This shouldn't be done like that. I ran that business for almost forty years. You've been there for a year and already you're running it into the ground," he says, mocking his father. Sweat begins beading up on his brow, and he wipes it away.

"Alright, calm down. We'll figure this out. Let me go down and tell Jazz to take care of my messages and cancel my appointments and I'll be back up to go over the files to see what we can do." I get up and walk back into my office to find Jazz still at her desk. She looks up when I walk in.

"Jazz, I need you to cancel all my meetings today, and if anyone calls, please take a message. I won't be in the office." I go back to my computer to shut it down.

"Do I need to stay here, or should I leave?"

I stand up and think it over. "Once the meetings are canceled, you can turn the machine on and go if you want. Take a day off; after yesterday, I'm sure you could use it."

She shrugs. "Thanks," she says, but her voice is off.

I stop what I'm doing and look over at her. "What's that?"

"You're just being nice today. It's weird."

I laugh and pick up my briefcase. "Yeah, I figured if we're going to work together, I should probably go easy on you. Enjoy your day." Without another word, I walk out.

5

JAZMINE

It doesn't take long to reschedule all the meetings. Within the hour, I'm clocked out and leaving the building. I pull out my cell phone and call Maddie.

"Hello?" she answers.

"I got the day off. Want to hang out?" I ask, walking up to the street and holding out my hand for a cab.

"Sure, there's a festival going on downtown. Want to check it out? We can get food on sticks. I know how much you like that."

I laugh. "Sounds good. I'll be at your place in a few."

"Okay, I'll get up and get dressed."

"You're still in bed? It's almost ten."

"Don't judge me," she says before hanging up the phone.

I laugh to myself and shake my head as I slide my phone into my purse.

A cab pulls over, and I slide into the backseat. I mumble off Maddie's address, and the car takes off. Instead of staring out the window, I open my new dating app and pull up the conversation from last night.

Jazz: *I got the day off and me and a friend are hitting up a festival downtown. Want to join?*

Brandon: *Wish I could, but I'm stuck at work. Another crisis that can't be handled without me. I hope you have fun though. And thanks for the invite.*

Jazz: *Maybe another time. I know we haven't talked much, but I hope to meet you one day. You seem like a great guy. Just please, don't turn out to be a serial killer j/k.*

Brandon: *I promise, when we come face to face, you'll be surprised, but it won't be because I'm a serial killer.*

Surprised? Why would I be surprised?

Jazz: *Why would I be surprised? You don't have two heads or anything, right?*

Brandon: *No! I'm completely normal, in a boring way. But I have a feeling we'll be great together. Have to get back to work. Feel free to send me some pictures of all the fun I'm missing.*

I smile to myself as I turn off the phone and put it back in its place. My mind immediately starts drifting off, imagining our first meeting. I picture us meeting one another on the street. Our eyes lock and we both freeze until we can form thoughts again. Slowly, we walk up to one another, meeting in the middle. He smiles and steals my breath. I lean in for a hug and feel his heart pounding.

"We're here, Miss," the driver says, breaking me from my thoughts.

"Oh, thanks." I quickly pass over the cash and climb out.

As I walk into the building, I find that my heart is racing just from imagining our first meeting. My breathing is fast, and my palms are sweaty. I laugh to myself. This is silly. I've only talked to the guy one time, and honestly, there is no proof that he even is a guy. I shouldn't let myself get this worked up. But there is something about him I find comforting. It feels like he's the one I'm meant to be with, like he's been with me all along. I can't for the life of me figure out why, though. This man that I've never met feels like home, like my past and future all held in one place. Half of my brain wants to run around screaming, *I finally found the one*, but the other half is saying I'm crazy for even thinking that so soon.

I let out a deep breath and shake my head at myself as I push through the door at Maddie's.

"Hey, what's up?" she asks, turning to look at me from her couch.

I drop my purse on the floor and zombie walk to the couch, collapsing beside her. "I'm so confused," I complain.

"About what?" she asks, pointing the remote at the TV and silencing it while giving me her full attention.

"Okay." I pull my legs up onto the couch and fold them beneath me. "Damon has been so hot and cold at work. Like, one minute he's checking me out, and the next he's using folders to build a fence between us. Then he's making out with some woman right in front of me but goes and tells me I'm cute. I don't know what kind of signals he's trying to throw at me, but it's getting confusing. So then, I thought I'll listen to Maddie and download that app because there's no better way to get over someone, right?" I ask, only pausing for a moment for her answer.

She nods.

"Well, I met this guy, and, Maddie, he's hot and sexy and kind of reminds me of Damon a little, but he has a sense of humor and doesn't try to torment me like Damon does. Something about this guy just reminds me of Damon so much, other than he's said some things I could never imagine Damon saying. I feel like I know him and I've never met him, and that's good and also bad. I mean, it's good because we clicked immediately, but it's bad because I'm already falling for this guy and I don't even know him." After my long, fast rant, I fall back against the cushions of the couch and take a deep breath.

"Okay, whoa, that was fast." Her blue eyes are wide, and her brows are lifted high. "Secondly, I get why you're so confused. But Jazz, I thought we talked about my brother?"

"I know," I cry.

"Look, I get that you've had a crush on him since, like, forever, but he's not the kind of guy you're looking for. My brother is a whore. And let's say he is starting to look at you differently, you know you'd just be like the rest of those girls. Do you really want that?" She looks down at me with sympathy.

"No," I reply.

"Okay, so you need to stop trying to analyze every little thing he says. If he flirts, it's probably just to watch you squirm, and if it's not for that reason, you'll end up heartbroken in the end anyway, and I'd hate to have to kill my stupid brother."

I nod in agreement.

"Now, as far as this other guy goes, it's okay to get excited. I mean, you haven't even met yet and already you're clicking like some people never do. So, be excited! But don't try and link him with Damon. He's not Damon, and he never will be. And that's not a bad thing. If Damon were that great, he would've scooped you up a long time ago. Just enjoy getting to know this guy and take it one day at a time. Okay?"

I nod. "Okay, you're right."

"Feel better now?"

I smile. "I do. I just needed everything out and put into perspective. Thanks, Maddie."

She smiles. "Now, let's go get day drunk and listen to live music." She throws the lap blanket off her legs and stands, looking me up and down. "But first, let's head to my closet to find you something a little more comfortable than work clothes, huh?"

I laugh. "Thank you! I wasn't even thinking about clothes when I came over here straight from work."

JAZZ: *How's it going?*

Brandon: *Good. How was the festival?*

Jazz: *Fun. Me and my best friend had a blast drinking craft beer and listening to all different kinds of music. I wish we could've met up, though.*

I quickly attach a picture Maddie had taken of me. In the pic, I'm smiling wide, eyes glazed over while holding two massive cups of beer.

Brandon: *Me too. It sounds fun. Being an adult sucks sometimes. I got stuck doing someone else's job today and had to work four hours later than normal.*

Brandon: *LOL love the pic! You're beautiful.*

My cheeks feel like they've been lit on fire, but I ignore his comment and instead reply to the message he sent before the picture loaded.

Jazz: *Yuck! I don't know why I was in such a hurry to grow up LOL*

Brandon: *Me either. I couldn't get you off my mind today. All day I caught myself daydreaming of you.*

My heart begins to pump harder, faster. I giggle to myself and pick up my glass of wine, taking a small sip.

Jazz: *I've thought about how our first meeting would go all day.*

Brandon: *And? What do you have in mind?*

Jazz: *I pictured a hundred different ways, but all of them ended the same.*

Brandon: *With a goodnight kiss, I hope.*

Jazz: *When can we finally meet? I hate to be so persistent, but I feel like I know you, like we're clicking better than anyone I've ever been with. It's a bit exciting, don't you think?*

Brandon: *I feel the same way. I'd love to meet up with you one of these days.*

It feels like I've been kicked in the stomach. One of these days? Why not today? Why not now?

Jazz: *Any idea when that will be?*

Brandon: *Things are crazy right now. I wish I could say that it would be soon, but I don't know for sure. I've been putting in so many extra hours that by the time I get home, I just fall into bed. But please don't take this as a sign that I don't want to meet, because I do. I really, really do.*

Jazz: *Okay, maybe I should slow down. I mean, we've only been talking for a day. We should get to know one another a little better first, that way when we do meet, it will be like we've known one another for years.*

Brandon: *I like the sound of that.*

Jazz: *Goodnight, Brandon.*

Brandon: *Goodnight, Jazmine.*

I WAKE in the morning with a pounding headache from drinking too much. I have to force myself to get out of bed, and I walk like a zombie to the bathroom. I don't wake up fully until I've stood under the hot water for a good ten minutes, but finally, I pull myself together enough to wash off before I'm late for work.

I blow dry my blonde hair and pull it into a sleek ponytail. I use a bit of concealer to hide my dark circles and add a little mascara and lip gloss. Finally, I pull on a pair of black dress pants, heels, and a light pink shirt. Grabbing all my things, I leave my apartment in a hurry.

When the cab pulls up in front of the building, I pay him quickly and look at my watch to see that I still have ten minutes left. I rush across the street for a cup of coffee and a muffin. I need the coffee to wake up, and the muffin to absorb some of this stomach acid left from drinking all night.

Walking into the office, I find Damon behind his desk looking as handsome and refreshed as ever.

"How was your day?" he asks with a smile, watching as I place my things on my desk and sit down.

"It was good. A little too good, actually. I'm a bit hungover, so if you could take it easy on me today, that'd be great." I take a sip of coffee and a bite of my muffin.

His smile widens. "I don't know why you think I *try* to give you a hard time.

I snort and roll my eyes. "You don't *try* to give me a hard time. It just comes naturally to you."

He stands, picks a folder up from his desk, and walks over to mine. He sits on the edge as he looks down at me with those dark, tempting eyes. "Per your request, I just have a few desk jobs for you to do today." He drops the folder in front of me. "I need this typed up and sent to every employee in the building. It's just some updated fine print."

I smile, happy that he's taking this seriously and not trying to make the day any harder on me. "Consider it done."

I immediately open the folder and start looking over the work but look up to find him sitting on my desk, still watching me.

"Is there anything else?" I ask, a little unsure of why he's still here, hovering over me.

"What would you say to grabbing some lunch today?"

His question confuses me. "You want me to run out and get your lunch?"

He laughs. "No. I mean, would you like to have lunch with me today?"

"Why? Is this work related?" I feel my face contort with confusion.

He lets out a deep breath and rubs his eyes. "No, Jazz. I just thought that since we're working together, we should get to know one another a little better as adults and work colleagues instead of as brother of the best friend and annoying little girl that pisses me off." He stands and clenches his teeth, making his angular jaw flex.

"Oh. Umm, okay. If you'd like." I nod.

His chest starts moving once again, making me realize that he's been holding his breath, awaiting my answer.

Without a word, he turns and walks back to his desk to sit down, and I turn my attention to the work at hand while picking at my muffin.

LUNCHTIME ROLLS around and Damon and I both walk out of the office together. We don't talk as we leave the building. I just follow along behind him and wonder what this is really about. Is he about to fire me? Is he buying me lunch to soften the blow and break the bad news? My heart has doubled its pace by the time we walk into the restaurant across the street.

He leads me to the back, and we sit at a booth across from one another. He picks up the menu, and I study him. While one hand holds the menu, the other is clenched into a fist so tight his knuckles are turning white. He's mindlessly biting his lower lip.

He's nervous.

I've never in my life seen Damon nervous. He's always so damn cocky and self-assured.

Seeing him this way only brings out my nervousness.

We both order a glass of water and I pick it up, drinking it down as fast as I can. He watches me with amusement in his eyes and a smile playing on his lips.

6

DAMON

Just sitting across from her causes my heart to double its pace. Sweat begins beading up on my skin, and there's this weird feeling in my gut. I'm nervous, but I have no idea why. I wish I could just come out and say what I'm thinking. I wish she would respond in a way that would make me happy, but I feel like if I told her how I'm really feeling, she'd laugh in my face. I mean, that's what I would do if I were her. I've done nothing but tease her for her entire life, and now I'm asking if she has feelings for me? Of course she doesn't.

"So, what's up, Damon? Is there something bothering you?"

There's plenty of things bothering me. In fact, two of those things are pointed right at me, rising and falling with her deep, even breathing.

I let out a breath, hoping to get control over my emotions, but it does no good. I'm more nervous than ever.

I shake my head. "No, nothing is bothering me. I just thought we could use this. I mean, I'm not exactly the guy that teased you growing up, and I know you're not the same little girl. I just thought that if we're going to be working together, maybe we need to get to know one another again. That's all." I shrug my shoulders, diverting my attention back to the menu in my hand, only now realizing that the other is clenched into a fist. I force it to relax. I'll take control of myself one body part at a time.

"Oh. Okay," she breathes out.

I look back up to see her relax into the booth.

"What?"

"I just thought you were bringing me here to fire me. I was a little worried." Her soft pink lips turn up in the corners.

"Why on earth would I fire you?" I level my eyes on hers.

"Well," she starts, leaning forward and adjusting herself in the seat. "We don't have the best relationship. I mean, we know one another, but we don't really know one another, if that makes sense."

I nod. "It makes perfect sense. That's why I wanted to take this afternoon to show you who I really am, and for you to show me just how much you've grown up." I grin at the thought.

She rolls her dark brown eyes and shakes her head. "Why does everything that comes out of your mouth sound like it has a double meaning?" she asks around a laugh.

I smile. "It usually does."

The waitress steps up to our table. "Can I start you two off with an appetizer?"

"I think I'd just like to order lunch," Jazz says, looking up at me.

I nod. "Me too."

"I'll take a cheeseburger and an order of cheese fries."

"That sounds good. Make it two, please," I add on, handing over the menu.

The waitress nods and walks away, leaving us alone and causing my heart to pick back up.

"So, what do you want to talk about?" Jazz asks, clasping her hands together as she watches me with wide eyes.

I clear my throat. "I don't know. What do you like to do?" It was the first question that popped into my head.

She frowns. "Shouldn't you already know this?"

"How would I know?"

"You've known me my whole life, Damon. You know me and your

sister go to every concert, comedy tour, and off-road show that comes to town. Why don't you tell me why we're really here, and stop pretending to care about any of this?"

I let out a deep breath and lean back in the booth. "Alright, I need some advice," I admit.

Her brows skyrocket. "Okay, what about?" She gains control over her features and seems genuinely interested.

"There's this woman," I start, and she scoffs, causing me to pause.

"Really? You need dating advice?" Her brows are pulled together, and her mouth is hanging open.

"No, I'm good at dating. But I haven't made it that far with this one yet. I'm too afraid to ask her out because I think she hates me."

This causes her to smile. "Nobody hates you, Damon. Well, maybe me, but that's it. You have charm for days. You're good-looking, you have a good job, and you're a nice guy when you're not trying to torture me."

I smile from hearing her compliments.

"Don't be so full of yourself." She crosses her arms and it causes her breasts to press together. I start seeing stars.

"I just don't know how to ask her. I mean, what should I say? What if it were you I was asking out? Forget our past. If I were a complete stranger and came up to you on the street, what would make you say yes?"

She sits back, picks up her water, and takes a drink while thinking it over. "Well, the complete stranger thing would be hard because I don't date anyone that I haven't formed some kind of bond with. But if there was a guy that I worked with or was friends with, I think the best way would be for him to surprise me. Like, just grab me and pull me in for a kiss. Make it fast and strong and passionate. Something I can't pull away from."

"Really?" I ask, surprised.

She laughs. "Absolutely. I'm a sucker for passion and romance." She points at me. "You do that, and you'll have her in the palm of your hand."

I smile. "Thanks for the tip."

Our food gets placed in front of us and we begin eating while the conversation drifts to a less stressful topic.

———

BY THE TIME we're walking back to the office, we're laughing and talking like old friends. We talk about concerts she's gone to, adventures I've taken, and she even tells me about the guy she's been talking to online. I want so badly to tell her that it's me, that I'm Brandon, but I don't. I feel like that's my way of talking to her without her seeing me. She can be honest with him, Brandon. He isn't the guy that teased her. Even if I can get her to take her walls down a bit, she still sees the boy I was, not the man I am.

I let her tell me about this guy, about how he seems to be the perfect match for her. I even talk more about the woman I'm having feelings for, but she never catches on, and it becomes clear I'm going to have to take her advice if I ever want this to go anywhere. But I'm nowhere near ready for that right now. Instead of making my move, we get back to work while I work up my courage.

While she works across the room from me, I can't help but to look up and watch her, watch the way she moves. She's absolutely gorgeous. I love the way she bites her lower lip, the way she twirls her blonde hair in between her fingers, and the way her dark eyes shine, and her lips turn up when she catches me staring.

When the day ends, I know I can't watch her walk out of this room not knowing. It's time. I have to make my move and see where it leads us. I have to let her know because it's killing me that she doesn't. I can't keep this to myself anymore.

I walk over to her desk and place a file folder on top. "Here's what you'll need in the morning."

She smiles sweetly. "Okay, I'll get to work on it first thing."

I nod once and watch as she turns around to pick up her purse from the floor beside her seat.

My feet seem to walk forward a couple steps but then back a few more. Then she turns around, and I freeze.

She smiles again. "I guess I'll see you in the morning?"

I return her smile and nod, suddenly losing my voice. I open my mouth, but no words come out.

"Okay, see ya," she says, stepping past me.

I spin around and watch as she gets closer and closer to that door, still not knowing.

Get a grip! You're blowing this. Do something. Say something. Just move!

Suddenly, all I see is a photo montage of her from over the years. Every smile from the time she was five years old until today. Something overcomes me. Love. These feelings aren't new. I've always had them. I've been in love with her from the moment my seven-year-old eyes met hers. I've just been too blind to see it. But something deep inside of me has always known it. Perhaps that's why I've picked on her and teased her all these years.

"Jazz," I call out, finally finding my voice as I push myself toward her.

"Yeah?" she asks, spinning around.

And the second she does, I'm pulling her against me. My lips find hers, and I kiss her deep, parting her lips with my tongue. She's frozen in shock and confusion. But the moment her chest mashes against mine and my tongue slide into her mouth, her body melts, and she kisses me back.

I walk her back a few steps, pressing her back against the wall while my tongue takes what it wants, what it needs. I burn everything into my memory, just in case she comes to her senses and smacks me silly. I want to remember her sweet taste, her soft lips, the way her warm body molds to mine. I want to remember the way my heart is pounding against my chest, the way I can feel hers pounding right alongside it. Everything inside of me wants everything inside of her, all of her.

My hands cup her cheeks, and her hands come up and cover mine. It takes several long seconds to realize that she wants this just as much as I do—she always has. Her chest is rising and falling heavily. Her breath blows against my cheek, and she lets out the softest of whimpers; it makes my dick harden and twitch with excitement.

This kiss was supposed to be long, hard, and slow. But I have lost all control. It's long and hard, but it's rushed, fueled with years of yearning, wanting, and needing. This kiss has taken on a life of its own. With every passing second, our hearts and souls only become more intertwined.

Her hands fall, landing on my chest as she gently pushes me backward. Our lips slow and break apart completely.

Her dark eyes meet mine, and already I can see the passion and lust burning in them. "This afternoon, it was me?"

"It's always been you, Jazz," I breathe out, closing the space between us once again. She kisses me back with just as much heat and electricity as before. My hands fall to her hips, lifting her up against me. Her legs wrap around my hips while her arms lace around my neck, pulling herself closer. Moving my hands to her ass for support, I move us to her desk, where I set her down. She lays back, and I bend over her. My aching dick presses to her center, and I grind it against her.

She lets out a deep, sexy moan and digs her nails into the back of my neck. Her reaction makes me do it again and again, but she stops.

"Wait, Damon."

I freeze, my heart and lungs still going at full speed as I pull away. I fall into her desk chair to regain control, and she sits up, adjusting her shirt that I've worked up.

"What is this? What's happening?" she whispers, eyes glued to the floor as if she's afraid to look at me.

I shake my head and let it fall back against the chair. "I can't do this anymore, Jazz. I can't see you every day and not have you."

"How long have you felt this way?" she asks, standing and pacing the floor in front of the desk.

"I don't know. I just know how I feel now, and how I've felt since you got here a few days ago."

She laughs, but it doesn't sound like a happy laugh. "This is so typical of you. I've been in love with you since I was five years old, and you tormented me. I had to watch you march in girl after girl. Hell, I just had to sit back and watch another woman kiss you right in front of me, and now you want me?" Her brows are drawn together, causing that cute little wrinkle to form between her eyes. "Well, it doesn't work this way, Damon. You don't get to treat me like trash my entire life, and then decide you want me." She grabs her purse off the floor where she dropped it.

"I never treated you like trash," I say, standing and marching toward her. "Did I tease you? Yes! Did I pick on you a little? Damn right, I did. But I only did those things because I liked you and didn't understand it or know what to do about it. Any time you've needed me, where have I been?" I ask, walking her backward until her back presses against the door.

"I've been right here, by your side. Even if you didn't know it. Even if you didn't want me to. I've been the big brother you never had. I damn near got expelled from high school when I kicked Martin Gregs' ass for you. And I didn't do that because you were my sister's best friend. I did that because I loved you."

"You were the one that beat up Martin Gregs?" she whispers.

I nod, walking forward until there is only an inch between us.

"Maddie, she never told me." Her eyes are wide with surprise as she gently shakes her head.

"I made her promise she wouldn't," I clip out.

"Why?" she asks, still breathless from our kiss.

"Why?" I ask, locking my eyes on hers. "Because I love you. You're the only one I ever wanted and the only one I couldn't have. I'm tired of not getting what I want, Jazmine."

"What did you expect me to say, Damon?" She steps forward, causing me to take a step back. "Did you think you'd profess your love and I'd fall right into your bed? Did you think finally hearing the words I've always dreamt of would allow you to treat me like another one of the women you fuck on your desk? Because that isn't me. It isn't going to happen. I refuse to be another one of your conquests."

"I didn't think that at all," I say in a rush.

"Damon, we both know how you wanted this day to go. Otherwise, I wouldn't have been spread open on that desk just now. I thought it was just a kiss, and I admit, it meant more to me than you will ever realize, but I never wanted to be another notch on your belt. If you love me like you say you do, you'll figure out how to make this right, because I've never been the girl that falls into bed with whatever guy is saying the right words."

7

JAZMINE

I pull my purse higher on my shoulder as I rush from the office. I hear the door open behind me, but I don't stop, and he doesn't call out to me. Instead, I rush to the elevator that opens as soon as I push the button. Stepping inside, I press the button for the ground level and look up. My eyes meet his. His hands are in his pants pockets, jacket held open. His jaw is cocked, eyes burning with anger and desire. Just as the doors begin to close, he swallows, causing his Adam's apple to bob in his throat.

When the elevator starts to descend, I lean against the wall. Closing my eyes, I take a deep, clearing breath. My heart is pounding uncontrollably, and my mind is an endless string of thoughts. I'm so confused and angry, but also giddy at the same time. Damon wants me? He's always been in love with me? I shake my head, too confused to figure anything out.

When the doors open, I rush from the elevator, almost afraid that he will catch up to me. I just need time to think and process. We can talk later about my feelings, his feelings, and the things that happened in his office. But right now, I need space. I need to get away. I need to think things through. And the only way I ever figure anything out is by sinking into a hot bath in my dimly lit bathroom with a glass of cold wine.

The ride home is a blur. I couldn't even tell you the cab number. That may not be a smart decision in Chicago. You're taught to always be aware of your surroundings, but I couldn't even tell you what the cabbie looked like. I'm too lost in thought.

I let myself into my apartment and lock the door behind me. I drop my things on the kitchen table and move to the fridge. Pulling out the bottle of wine, I grab a glass and pour it full. I pick it up and drink it quickly, letting the ice-cold liquid relax my worries.

When the glass is gone, I'm left breathless. Instead of pouring another, I pick up the bottle and take it with me to the bathroom. It's clear that if I need to function, I can't think about any of this. So, I clear my head and focus on filling the tub with water and bubbles. I light a dozen candles and scatter them around the room, then turn on the radio that's on the shelf in the corner. I turn it up loud enough that I can hear it over the water but keep it low enough so I can still hear my thoughts.

Finally, I strip off my clothes and slide into the deep tub. I breathe in deeply and smell the relaxing scent of lavender and vanilla. I slide down until I can lay my head back and close my eyes. Immediately, his face pops into my head. I let out a pouting sound, still confused. I want to call Maddie and tell her all of this, but I know she would say not to fall for it, that he's only using me. She doesn't know how hard it is to not fall for it. There's one thing I've wanted my entire life, and now it's being offered to me. Why is it so bad to just take it?

Because you know it won't last and you'll be heartbroken, I tell myself.

But what if I can keep myself in check? If I know it's only fun and games, why is it bad to enjoy it?

My phone chimes, interrupting my thoughts.

I turn my head and see that I've left it sitting on the sink next to the open bottle of wine.

With a groan, I stand and stretch far to pick them both up. Sitting back down in my bubbly water, I take a drink and check the notification on my phone. It's a message from Brandon.

Brandon: *Hi, beautiful. How was your day?*

I smile from reading his message.

Jazz: *Crazy. Confusing. How was yours?*

Brandon: *What happened, if you don't mind me asking.*

Jazz: *Remember that guy I told you I've always had a thing for? He told me he's been in love with me too. And he kissed me. It was an amazing kiss. We both got a little too caught up, and it almost went further. But then I remembered my best friend's warning. I'm afraid that if I take this step with him, I'll get lost and end up hurt.*

Brandon: *Oh, wow. That is confusing, isn't it? I understand everything you're going through. It's like you finally get what you've always wanted, but it's not 'how' you want it. The question is: do you take it anyway, or punish yourself because it didn't come when/how you wanted it to?*

Reading his message makes me let out a long breath and take another drink. He's right. Even though I'm supposed to be getting to know this guy to date, he's giving me relationship advice, advice that means it will never happen for the two of us. But it also makes me realize that I shouldn't pass on this just because it took Damon longer to find his feelings than it did me.

Jazz: *You're right. I shouldn't push this away because it wasn't on my terms. I should just be glad that I'm getting what I've always wanted.*

Brandon: *I hope everything works out for you and hope the girl that I've secretly been in love with comes around as your dream guy has.*

Jazz: *But if I follow this road, it means we'll never meet.*

Brandon: *If it's meant to be, we'll meet. Maybe we have to date all the wrong people so we know when we've found the right one.*

I smile and shut off my phone, dropping it into the floor beside the tub. I take another drink of wine and lean my head back. Closing my eyes after drinking so much in such a short time has me feeling dizzy and at ease.

Suddenly, I hear someone banging on my door. The loud noise makes me jump, the bubbles sloshing over the edge of the tub. I quickly stand up and wrap myself in my fluffy robe. I place the half-empty bottle of wine on the counter and rush through the kitchen and to the front door. I look into the peephole and see Damon.

A deep breath leaves me as I unlock the door and pull it open.

He rushes inside like he's afraid I'll never let him in.

"I'm sorry, Jazz. I didn't mean for things to go the way they did. I just lost control when I finally got to kiss you. I was just so excited that you didn't smack me, that you wanted to kiss me back. All this time I thought you hated me, so learning that you were feeling the same way, it was just overpowering." His chest is heaving, and his dark hair is a mess that's falling into his eyes. He's breathtaking.

"Damon," I say, hoping to end his rant.

He shakes his head as he walks closer. "I can't promise that this will be perfect. But I can promise that I won't purposely do anything to hurt you. I'm not using you. I'm not trying to fuck you and forget you." He's only a few inches away now, and I keep my eyes locked on his as I reach out and pull his mouth to mine.

The kiss effectively stops his talking, and his hands wrap around my hips, pulling me closer as his tongue dives into my mouth and dances with my own. My fingers lace into his dark hair, gently tugging and pulling. Before I'm ready, he breaks the kiss and steps back. His mouth is open like he's going to say something, but I think for the first time in his life, he's speechless.

I laugh and shake my head but take a step forward until our lips are welded together once again. He pulls away completely, putting several feet between us.

"I want more with you, Jazz. I know the impression I gave you earlier, and it was unintended. I don't just want sex. I want all of you."

I nod and bite my lower lip. A part of me wants to believe him, but there's another part that doesn't want to believe him because it doesn't want to be hurt and let down. So no matter what he says, I'm going to treat this as a fling, something that isn't made to last.

As he continues to tell me how seriously he's taking this, I look down to see my body covered in a robe. Slowly, I move my hands to the sash keeping it closed. At first, it doesn't register with him what I'm doing, but the second my robe is open completely, his mouth snaps shut and his jaw twitches.

I watch as his green-blue eyes start at my feet and move slowly up my body. The moment my robe hits the floor, I find myself in his strong arms with his mouth against mine. Even though his mouth is moving against mine, forcefully and rushed, his hands are holding my hips respectfully. They're not roaming my body, grabbing anything they can. He's holding my body close to his; he's cherishing, protecting.

Suddenly, he breaks the kiss. "I'm a fucking saint," he mutters as he snatches my robe off the floor.

"What are you—" I start, just as he swings it around and covers me back up.

His green eyes lock on mine. "You said earlier I needed to find a way to prove to you that I'm not just using you for sex, so this is it. I can taste a bottle of wine on your tongue. You don't get to seduce me into sex that you will blame on being drunk later. When we get together, I promise, you will want it, and there's no way you will say it's a mistake."

After I slide my arms into the sleeves, he ties the sash tightly.

"Now that we're on the same page, I'm going to leave, and I will see you tomorrow." He spins around for the door.

My mouth drops open. "But..."

He stops and looks back at me with a forced smile. "Goodnight, Jazmine." Without another word, he lets himself out.

A laugh slips past my lips. I'm surprised, to say the least, but I'm happy he did what he did. It would've been too easy for me to sleep with him tonight. And, I'm sure, I would have been second guessing and over analyzing it tomorrow. Maybe he knows me better than I thought.

I lock the door and go back into the bathroom to blow out the candles and drain the tub. Taking my bottle of wine to the bedroom with me, I shrug out of my robe and slip into bed.

My phone dings and I open a message from Damon. It's just a picture of a blue ball. I laugh until my eyes water, then reply.

Jazz: *I'm sorry. You were right. I would have regretted it in the morning. Or, at least, made things awkward.*

Damon: *But showing me your beautiful naked body and letting me leave with blue balls won't make things awkward? LOL*

Jazz: *Let's just hope I'm drunk enough that I won't remember.*

Damon: *You better not forget. What will I need to do to remind you?*

Jazz: *I won't forget a kiss like that, Damon.* Just admitting that makes me blush.

Damon: *Me either, Jazz. I hope you know I'm in this for the long haul now. You thought I was relentless before? Haha, you haven't seen anything yet.*

I smile as I shut off the phone and roll to my side. I'm glad I didn't sleep with Damon. I mean, it would have gone against everything I said in his office. I've never been the kind of girl that falls in bed with anyone. I'm glad I didn't start with him.

Even though I'm glad we didn't have sex, that doesn't mean I can't think about us having sex. I fall asleep quickly and dream of us becoming one for the first time.

I WAKE in the morning and have forgotten all about last night. I push myself up from the bed and find that I'm completely naked. Sleeping naked isn't something I usually do, then I remember yesterday at the office: Damon kissing me and laying me down across my desk. I remember the bath and the wine. I remember him coming over and how I dropped my robe for him to see my whole body. My face heats up and blush stains my face.

Oh, God. Why did I do that? I don't know if I should be happy Damon stopped it or be upset because he denied me. I force all thoughts away and focus on getting ready for work. I dress in a gray skirt with a white top and leave my hair hanging down my back in loose curls. I apply a small amount of makeup and grab my phone and purse. The moment I'm stepping outside, I see I have a text from Damon.

Damon: *I'm taking you to work today. I'm at the curb.*

I look up from my phone and see his black Jeep Wrangler. I smile to myself and walk over. Before I can close the distance, he steps out, holding a bouquet of flowers and a cup of coffee.

My smile widens. "What is all this?"

He shrugs. "I thought you might need a little pick-me-up after all your wine last night."

I laugh but thank him. I'm taking my first sip when he opens my door for me. I slide into the seat and find a pink bakery box.

He climbs behind the wheel and picks up the box, opening it to reveal blueberry muffins.

I laugh. "You don't have to do all of this, Damon."

"What am I doing?"

"You're doing all these things you wouldn't normally do to keep my mind off the embarrassment from last night."

"Who's embarrassed?" he asks, closing the box and setting it down between us.

"I am! I mean, I said I wasn't the type of girl that falls into bed, and then that's exactly what I tried to do with you. And you rejected me! Who wouldn't be embarrassed about that?"

He holds up his finger to stop me from talking. "I didn't reject you. I just stopped you from making a drunk decision you may have regretted later. Do I want to have sex with you? Hell yes, I do, but I also want more. And that is why I'm more than willing to wait as long as you see fit."

I roll my eyes. "Do you really think this is a good idea?" I motion between the two of us.

I see him let out a long breath just before he leans over and pulls me in for a long, slow kiss. Something about this kiss causes all of my thoughts to stop. I can't do anything but kiss him back and, mentally, give teenage me a high five.

He pulls back slightly but keeps his hands on my cheeks, so I have to maintain eye contact. "Stop, Jazz. If there's one thing I know about you, it's that you overthink everything. Just let yourself go. Nobody has to know what we're doing right now. Let's just see where we end up. If we end up together for the rest of our lives, then great. But if for some reason, things don't work out, no hard feelings. It won't change anything between us at work or around our families. Deal?"

I nod once. "Deal," I agree.

He gives me his breathtaking smile and one last, quick kiss. "Now, let's get to work. I hear your boss is a real tight-ass."

I can't hold back my laugh. "You have no idea. He made me staple four-hundred pages together the other day."

He scoffs but shifts into drive and hits the gas.

8

DAMON

I'm sitting at my desk, trying to focus on work. But I can't. All I can do is watch her. She's standing at the far end of the room, filing papers, and I can't take my eyes off that round ass. She sways from side to side, trying to get comfortable in those impossible shoes she insists on wearing. With every sway of her hips, I regret walking out on her last night. I know I did the right thing, but fuck, I am a saint.

I clear my throat and force my eyes back to the computer. But the sound of a drawer opening has my eyes right back across the room where she's now bending over to file papers in the bottom of the cabinet.

I don't remember moving across the room, but the next thing I know, I have her back to those filing cabinets and her mouth against mine. Her breath is sweet, a mixture of coffee and blueberries. And her lips are soft, warm, and inviting. My hand on her hip moves lower, grabbing a handful of her plump ass and squeezing. She lets out a soft whimper and my dick twitches.

"Damon," she whispers.

"I know, I know," I say, forcefully removing myself from her.

She giggles and it makes my stomach muscles tighten. "Didn't take care of your little problem last night, huh?"

I let out a deep chuckle. "Oh, I did. Once in the shower last night to get that body of yours off my mind, and once again this morning to keep my head in the game today. Neither worked very well," I say, moving back toward her. My lips almost touch hers, but she holds up her finger between us, making me freeze and want to cry all at once.

"I think if we're going to do this, someone needs to get busy planning a date." She smiles, being the ornery ass she is.

"Are you saying I can't kiss you until I take you out on a date?"

"No, I'm saying you can't touch me until you take me out on a date."

Even though I have her partially blocked between me and the filing cabinet, she slips past me, picks up more papers, and bends over to file them.

I groan and clench my hands into fists. I stand back and watch her bend over. Every time, she looks over her shoulder and smiles at me, teasing me even further. I bring my fist up to my mouth and bite down on it. This only makes her giggle.

Someone knocks on the door, and I have to almost run to take a seat at my desk so whoever walks in doesn't see the massive erection I have right now.

Jazz walks over to the door and opens it. Maddie walks inside, making me roll my eyes.

"What are you doing sitting down over there while my best friend works her butt off?" she asks, walking closer to my desk.

"She ain't doing anything but filing papers. Trust me; I like watching that ass. I don't want it to go anywhere." I send Jazz a grin and a wink, to which she scoffs and rolls her eyes.

Maddie glances between Jazz and me before walking over to her and whispering something in her ear. Jazz agrees quickly, and they both turn back to me.

"What are you two cooking up over there?"

Maddie comes walking over with a grin, meaning she's up to something. "I just came up to tell Jazz about a bunch of us getting together tonight to hit up the club. You know, just a way for all the staff to gather and talk shit about you higher-up people. But I'm going with Travis and was worried that Jazz wouldn't be able to find a date in time. But I'm sure you wouldn't mind taking her, considering how much you like to watch that ass of hers, right?"

I glance back and forth between the two, unsure of what to say. Hell yeah, I'd like to take Jazz to a club so she can shake her ass on me all night, but we've agreed to keep things under wraps for a while.

"I don't know about all that," I say, getting nervous.

"You just said so, didn't you?" she raises a brow.

"I was just messing around. You know how I like to make Jazz uncomfortable. I've recently found out that she has nothing to say when it comes to hitting on her." I laugh, even though it's completely true. Nothing bothered her more than me hitting on her.

"Meet us there at seven," she says, spinning around toward the door and looking at Jazz.

Jazz shrugs in agreement.

"I didn't say I'd go!" I shout after her. She ignores me and rushes out the door anyway.

I look back over at Jazz, questions written all over my face. "How's this going to work?"

She shrugs. "What do you mean?"

"I thought we were keeping this quiet for now? And now I have to take you to a club and watch you shake your ass all night without touching you?"

She giggles. "Guess so. If I were you, I'd set up some dinner plans and turn this into a date in a hurry. Or you may end up with blue balls two nights in a row." Without another word, she leaves the office, leaves me speechless and staring after her.

———

It's six o'clock when I'm knocking on Jazmine's door. She quickly cracks it but doesn't pull it open.

"Jazz?" I ask, pushing the door open to find an empty kitchen.

"I'm not ready yet. Make yourself at home and I'll be out in a sec," she yells from somewhere in the apartment.

I walk in and close the door behind me. "Should I come back? We're supposed to be at the club at seven." I walk through the kitchen into the living room.

"No, almost done. We'll have just enough time to grab a quick dinner."

I don't reply as I walk around, looking over all the pictures she has of our childhood. There's one picture of all of us on prom night. There's me with my date, a bottle blonde, but I'm not looking at the camera or my date: I'm looking at Jazz standing right next to me. Jazz looks elegant and beautiful, even for a freshman. She and my sister weren't even old enough to go, but they both went with older guys that were juniors at the time. My eyes land on Martin Gregs, and the memory of that night plays out in front of my eyes.

The dance is over, and we're all at the after party. I begged my sister and Jazz just to go home, they're too young to be here. But of course, they didn't listen. They want the full high school experience.

I've left my annoying date back in the room. She's way too drunk, and after getting puke on my shoes, I'm out. I've found her a ride home with one of her friends, so now I plan on finding Maddie and Jazz and getting them the fuck out of here.

I walk into the back yard of the mansion, and there are people making out in every seat; nearly the whole senior class is naked in the pool. I bump into Jordan, a guy that is on the wrestling team.

"Hey, have you seen my sister and Jazz?"

He laughs. "Your sister is over there, doing body shots with her date, and Jazz," he smiles wide, "she just went upstairs with Martin."

My eyes double in size. "She went upstairs?"

He nods. "Yeah, she's pretty drunk. So is your sister. I'm pretty sure their dates are trying for something, if you get what I mean."

Fuck. I push myself forward. I rush past the pool and all the people yelling at me to come party when them and into the pool house where they're handing out drinks and doing shots. I find Maddie and rush up to her. She's so drunk she's barely standing on her own.

"Time to go, Mads." I grab ahold of her arm and tug her in my direction. She stumbles, and her douche of a date catches her.

"Whoa, she ain't ready to go anywhere. Are ya, babe?" He looks down at her.

She looks up at him with a big smile. "No, I'm fine, Damon. Mark will take me home."

"Yeah, it's no problem," he says, pulling her back to his lap.

"Like hell you will," I tell him, walking closer.

He stands so we're eye to eye.

"Take your hands off my sister before I rip them off of you. Playing college ball will be pretty hard with no hands." I shove against his chest, and he falls into his seat.

He looks up at Maddie. "Get lost," he tells her, using a bitter tone for the first time tonight, now that he knows he's not getting lucky with my little sister.

I take her arm and tug her from the pool house.

"Wait! Where's Jazz?"

"We're going for her next. Apparently, she thought it'd be a good idea to go to a bedroom with Gregs."

She giggles loud. "Jazz is going to get laaaiiiddd!" she cheers.

"Over my dead body," I mumble under my breath.

We make our way to the second floor and stop at the end of the long hallway. There are at least ten doors on each side.

"How are we going to know which room they're in? It's not like you're going to march into everyone," Maddie says, leaning against the wall.

I go door to door, putting my ear against each one. I hear party sounds in some rooms, moaning in others, then finally get to one where I hear muffled whispers.

"No, stop," a girl says, but I can't tell if it's Jazz.

"Just relax, Jazz. It won't hurt. I promise."

"I said stop!" she yells.

That's all I need to hear. I take a few steps back and jam my shoulder into the door. The wood splinters and cracks, but the door flings open.

Martin is rolling all over her. Her red dress is worked up over her hips, *and her makeup and hair are a mess. His head pops up, and he stands. "Hey, man. It wasn't what it sounded like. Tell him, Jazz."*

I push him, and he falls onto the bed. I hold out my hand, and she takes it, and I pull her into my side. I walk her from the room with tears running down her red cheeks.

There's no way I'm done with that mother fucker, but first, I have to get Jazz someplace safe and warm.

I'll be back.

"I'm ready. What do you think?" Jazz asks, breaking me from my memories.

I turn around and find her standing in front of me, looking gorgeous in a short black dress. It hugs every single curve on her body and has her long legs and upper chest on display. Her blonde hair is pulled half up, so her beautiful face is clear to see, but the rest hangs down her back in soft, flowing curls. She's wearing more makeup than I think she needs, eyes darkly lined, and lips painted a bright red, but most girls overdo it on makeup for a night of dancing. And it doesn't take away from her natural beauty. Just seeing her this way and knowing that she'll be in my arms all night, I'm already excited and straining against my jeans.

"Wow. You look amazing," I manage to get out.

"You think so? It's not too much?" she spins in a circle, and I get a full view of every curve I want to touch, and kiss, and lick.

"No way. I think I'm going to have a hard time keeping the guys away from you tonight." I move closer and pull her against me. "Guess I'll just have to let them know who you belong with." I move in for a kiss.

She kisses me quickly but breaks it off. "Nope, we can't be a couple in front of Mads," she says, wrapping her arms around my neck.

I look to the ceiling and groan. "Ugh, what the fuck? Let's blow off the club." I bring my eyes back to hers, moving in for another kiss, but she's not having it.

"I would love to, but we can't leave Maddie there alone. We don't know anything about this guy she's bringing."

"Fine, let's grab a quick dinner and go to the club so we can get back to our date."

She smiles. "Do you have anything planned?" she asks, releasing me and walking past me into the kitchen, toward the door.

"I guess you'll just have to wait and find out," I tease, trying my damnedest to think of something.

WE'RE both sitting in my Jeep outside the club, trying to eat our dinner. Jazz insisted on grabbing some trash from a hotdog cart, so now we both have a soda, chips, and messy-ass hotdogs that we're trying to keep from dripping on our clothes and the seats.

"I can't believe you eat this stuff," I complain, wiping mustard from my lip.

She laughs. "We didn't have a lot of time. Next time, I'll let you pick the place." She smiles and winks at me before taking a bite of her hotdog.

I laugh and shake my head. "I've never seen a woman in a cocktail dress scarfing down a hotdog."

She shrugs one shoulder. "Hang with me and you'll see all kinds of things."

We finish with our food and climb out of the Jeep. I want to reach over and take her hand, but I remember I can't. I let out a sigh that gets her attention, but she doesn't ask what it's about. I have a feeling she already knows.

After all this time, it's finally okay to touch her, and yet in this moment I can't touch her. It's infuriating.

We're stopped at the door, and we both show our licenses before we're allowed inside. The loud music and deep bass hit us the second we walk in, and the door closes behind us, shielding us in the darkness.

We both pause, looking around the place. Multicolored lights flash all around the room, and neon bar signs light the walls. In the front portion of the building are a couple of pool tables and the bar.

The rest of the big room has smaller tables and booths and a massive dance floor. Everything is done in black and silver.

"Want a drink?" I ask, placing my hand on the bend of her arm.

She smiles and nods.

We sit down at the bar, and I order a beer while she orders some fruity mixed drink.

"Going right for the hard stuff, huh?"

"I don't drink beer. It's nasty." She scrunches her nose.

"I seem to remember many times I've caught you drunk off your ass from drinking keg beer."

Her cheeks redden. "I've learned my lesson. Especially after that time I laid in a field and puked my guts up all night."

My back straightens as I turn to face her. "When was that?"

"My senior year. You were already gone to college." She picks up her drink and takes a sip.

I shake my head from hearing her story and hand over some cash for our drinks. Picking up my beer, I take a long drink. "And here I was thinking I've always been around to save you."

"You have. All it took was Maddie threatening to call you to make me get up," she laughs out.

I smile. "I would've chewed your ass out." She knows it's the truth too. Every time I caught them doing something stupid or dangerous, I was the one getting onto them. I didn't need to run to the parents and have them grounded.

"I know. That's why I got up," she says around a laugh. "I didn't need you showing up and throwing me over your shoulder. That one time was enough."

I shrug and laugh. "Well, you shouldn't have lied to me. You guys had no business going to that college party when you were seventeen."

"I was dating a guy in college. It was his party."

"I know," I say with a big smile. "And that didn't stop me from walking into his room and pulling you out from under him, did it?"

She rolls her eyes. "I have a question," she says quietly, dark eyes narrowing on me.

"What's that?" I lean forward.

"All these years I've thought that you busting in when I got too close with a guy was your way of protecting me."

I nod. "It was."

"Was it? Or was it because deep down, you were jealous?"

9

JAZMINE

My question makes him uneasy. I can tell because his mouth opens and snaps shut without making a sound. He picks up his beer bottle and finishes it off, then turns toward me, more prepared to answer.

"I wouldn't say I was jealous. I was protecting you, taking care of you because I knew you didn't have a brother or a dad to do it. I treated you like my sister: no guy is good enough. But yeah, it pissed me off when I found out you were getting too close with another guy because... you were mine. You are mine." His blue eyes level on me, and they cut right through me, forcing me to hold my breath. "Always have been and always will be," he says, taking his eyes off me and motioning for another drink.

After he gets another beer, he looks over at me to find me still frozen by his words. He smirks, and his eyes slowly drift down my body. He quickly looks around, not finding Maddie or anyone from work. He takes my hand to dance.

"What? Wait, what about Maddie?"

"She's not here yet. I bet if we go into that far corner, nobody will even see us. Come on." He takes my hand and drags me across the dance floor, over into the far corner the lights don't hit. He spins around and pulls me to his chest. My breasts press against him, and our eyes lock as he moves against me. My lips part with my heavy breathing.

"What's the matter, Jazmine?" he asks low in my ear.

I shake my head clear. It's obviously clouded with too many dirty thoughts.

I feel his lips press against my neck, and my eyes flutter closed. It's been too long since I've been close to someone. His hot mouth feels too good on my neck.

He slowly works his way up my neck and to my ear, where he bites gently. His hot breath blows against my cheek, lighting me on fire. A sigh leaves my lips, and he pulls back to study my face.

"You have no idea what that sound does to me, do you?"

"What sound?"

"That soft gasp and quiet whimper. You do that every time we get close."

"Do I? I never noticed it before."

"You've never made that sound when another man's touched you or kissed you?" he asks, green eyes darkening.

I shake my head once. "Never."

Before I can process what's happening, I find my back to the wall and his lips to mine. His tongue teases my every thought. I should push him away—we're in public. But I don't. I can't. I want him, and it's nothing like last night. Now, it's real. It's an ache in my stomach. It's a throbbing pain between my thighs. I can feel it every time my heart beats, with every breath I take. I need to feel him inside me. I want his weight crushing me into the bed. I need to hear his moans and gasps that are only intended for me.

My hand moves to his waistband and my fingers hook his jeans, pulling him closer. When my hand begins to slide down the front, he breaks the kiss.

"What are you doing?" he asks in an amused tone.

"I don't want to wait anymore. We've had twenty years of foreplay. I think that's enough, don't you?"

When he doesn't answer, I ask, "My place or yours?"

He snickers under his breath. "What about Maddie?"

Hearing Maddie's name reminds me of why we're here to begin with. "Fuck," I whisper. "We can't stand her up."

I pull my hand away before I even touch what I so desperately need. I quickly glance around, finding a few people that we work with but not Maddie.

"I guess we should get over there." I point at the table with familiar faces.

He places his hand flat on my stomach and gently pushes me back against the wall. "Or I could slide my hand up under this dress of yours and give you something to look forward to." His hand starts trailing up my inner thigh.

I've never been one to create a public display, but his hand feels too good. I can't stop it. His fingers barely brush against my sex when he pulls it away. My eyes snap open and lock on his to see his grin.

"On second thought, I think I'll make you wait it out like I have to."

I roll my eyes and smack his chest before walking off and leaving him to follow along after me.

I stop at the bar and order a fresh drink, then head over to the table just as Maddie and another guy come walking in.

"Jazz!" she screams, running up to me and pulling a guy with tan skin and blond hair up behind her. She quickly gives me a hug. "This is Travis. Travis, this is my best friend Jazmine, and this is my brother, Damon."

I turn around in time to see Damon come to a stop just behind me. He holds out his hand.

"Nice to meet you," Travis says, shaking his hand.

"Don't make me kick your ass. This is my baby sister. Understand?"

He nods as he glances between Maddie and Damon, but then excuses himself to order their drinks.

Maddie grabs my bicep and pulls me over to the table. "So, how did you talk my stupid brother into bringing you?"

I shrug. "I'm just as surprised as you are. He just showed up at my door. I was already dressed and planning on coming alone. I guess I made him feel guilty earlier talking about how lonely I'd be sitting here by myself." I laugh.

"Good. He needs to get out. And I'm much happier having him here with you than finding some whore to take home."

I force a smile. "Yeah, I'll keep him good and single for you."

Her eyes widen. "Not for me; for him. He doesn't need to be messing with all these females the way he has been. He's going to end up with a disease."

We both laugh. Damon takes the seat next to me. "What's so funny?"

"Nothing," Maddie and I say in unison.

A FEW HOURS and many drinks later, everyone is up and dancing. We're having a good time. Well, everyone but Damon, who sits at the table drinking beer after beer. I can see that it's driving him crazy having to sit there and watch everyone having fun, but he refuses to dance with me because he's scared that Maddie will think it's weird and put the pieces together.

Maddie turns, so her back is facing Damon. "You know, you may be on to something."

"What do you mean?"

"The other day when you said Damon has been looking at you differently. I've been watching him tonight, and he hasn't taken his eyes off you."

I wave her off. "No, he's probably just making sure I don't get into trouble like I used to. You know how many guys he's beat up because he thought they were being too handsy."

She shakes her head. "I don't think so. Let's test my theory. Go ask him to dance."

"I already have. At least ten times already."

"No, I mean, go over to him and dance on him, pull him to the floor. I'll pretend not to pay attention." Without another word, she dances off.

I stop dancing and walk over to the table. I sit down and pick up my drink. Holding it in front of my mouth, I say, "Maddie's testing a theory."

"What theory is that?" Damon asks with a grin. He knows his sister is always up to something.

"She's noticed the way you've been looking at me all night. She wants to see if you'll dance with me."

He laughs. "Well, let's give her a show." He grabs my hand pulls me out on the dance floor, spinning me around and into his arms. When we're chest to chest with our arms around one another, he whispers, "There, that's better."

His body moving against mine has me hot as hell. He has one knee in between my legs, and every time he moves his hips, his hard cock rubs against me, only making it worse.

His eyes find mine, and I can see the desire burning in his green eyes. I think he can see it burning in mine as well because he pulls away, looks at his watch, and says, "I need to get going."

I nod. "Me too," I agree.

We both walk over to the table and finish our drinks. Maddie comes running over.

"Aw, are you guys taking off. It's only ten!"

"Yeah, I have too much to do in the morning to stay out late getting trashed," Damon says, putting his empty bottle on the table.

"What about you?" she asks me. "We can give you a ride home later."

I wave my hand through the air, dismissing the thought. "Thanks, but I'm tired. Plus, I don't want to be your third wheel. This is, what, the fourth date with Travis? I'm sure you guys need your alone time."

"Okay, call me tomorrow?" she asks, pulling me in for a hug.

"Of course."

"You better be careful with this guy. Call if you need me," Damon says, looking directly at her, letting her know that he's serious.

She smiles and waves as we pass her by, heading for the doors.

The second we step outside and the cool air hits us, Damon takes my hand and pulls me into his arms, his lips landing on mine. My eyes are closed, and I'm completely lost, but I feel the cool metal of the Jeep against my back. His hands are in a rush to touch every spot he can. They run up my thighs and squeeze my ass, move up over my hips and to my breasts. He gently massages them, making me whimper softly.

He pulls away, green eyes locking with mine. "Let's get going before you make me explode." He pulls us away from the Jeep so he can open my door. I jump in without argument.

———

We don't speak on the drive to his house—the closest of our two places. The second he pulls into the drive, he throws it into park and jumps out. By the time I have my seatbelt off, my door is being swung open, and he's pulling me into his arms.

It's dark, only the light of the moon shining down and a couple of streetlights at the end of the block, so I'm not worried about anyone seeing my ass that's now hanging out of my dress from having my legs wrapped around his hips as he carries me to the door.

His mouth never leaves mine, and his tongue never stops dancing —even as he uses the keys in his hand to unlock the door. Finally getting in, he kicks the door shut behind us and turns us around until I feel the hardwood pressed to my back. He sets me on my feet and pulls off his leather jacket, dropping it into the floor as I work on his belt.

His strong hands land on my hips, one pulling me closer while the other pulls down the zipper in the back of my dress. I tug off his belt and toss it into the floor while he starts pulling down my dress. Once he gets it below my ass, it falls to my feet, where I step out of it and kick it off to the side. He pulls away, chest heaving and eyes flooded with passion.

"There's something about you that makes me want to lose all control," he pants out between labored breaths.

I'm just as breathless. I can't form words, but I agree by nodding my head. I know I've known Damon my entire life, but this is our first date. Here I am, ready to jump into bed with him. But things are different with Damon. Maybe it's because he's been my protector my whole life. I know he would never do anything to hurt me. He's fought too long and too hard to see me broken now.

He picks me back up, and I latch on around his neck as he walks us through the house.

"I hope you don't have any place to be because I'm taking my time with you." He drops me onto the bed, and I squeal. "I've missed out on touching you for the last twenty years. I'm making up for that tonight," he says in a deep voice I've never heard him use. The ceiling light isn't on, but there's a small lamp beside the bed. It shines bright enough to see around the room and everything he's doing. He's standing directly in front of me, slowly kicking off his boots and removing his clothing, down to a tight-fitting pair of blue boxer-briefs. I lick my lips in anticipation.

Instead of waiting for him to join me on the bed, I get myself to my knees and press a soft kiss to his collarbone. The moment my lips touch his skin, he sucks in a long breath. I look up and meet his eyes for only a second before pressing another kiss lower. I work my way over his pecks, down his abs, and to the waistband of his boxers. I pull away and look up at him for permission as my hands push his boxers down his hips. His erection springs free, long, thick, and standing at attention.

I place my hand at the base, working it back and forth as I wet my lips and lower my mouth to him. Already, a drop of dew is beading up on the end, and I lick it off before taking him into my mouth completely. He lets out a deep moan, and his right hand flies to my hair. He gently tugs it, egging me on. I take him deeper and deeper, wanting to please him. I swirl my tongue around the tip when I slide him out of my mouth before repeating the process over and over.

Doing this for him, it only makes me want him more. I want to hear all of his sounds. I want to taste his excitement. I want him calling my name in pleasure. And I want to remember every single second of it.

"Jazz, you have to stop," he says, barely above a whisper.

But I don't. I want to keep going. I need to push him over the edge. I need this. I've waited all these years; nobody is stealing this from me. Instead of stopping, I double my efforts. I suck harder; I move quicker. The second I send him a little too far back and I gag, he lets go. His hips start to thrust, and his breathing gets erratic. He moans loud and deep. And finally, he spills every last drop into my mouth, which I swallow with pride.

I sit back on my knees while he stands over me, panting and calming down.

"You're a bad girl, Jazmine." He places his hand under my jaw and tilts my head back. "I told you to stop, and you kept going."

I lick my lips and nod once. "I had to. I needed to."

"Why?" he asks, climbing onto the bed, causing me to lay back.

He hovers over me, holding my cheek softly.

"I've imagined doing that for you since I was old enough to know what it was. I wanted to hear my name fall from your lips. I wanted to taste your excitement and know that it was all because of me. That I made you feel that good."

He closes his eyes and kisses me softly as his hand moves to my throat. He doesn't squeeze, but it excites me knowing that he could.

"Now it's my turn," he whispers against my lips. He releases my neck and replaces his hand with his mouth, pressing soft kisses to my skin, working his way lower. When he gets to the swell of my breast, he unhooks my bra, and I bounce free. He looks deeply into my eyes before sucking my hard nipple into his mouth. He swirls his tongue around it, flicks against it, and massages my breast until he moves to the next. With his hands cupping me and rubbing me, his mouth descends even lower. Down my stomach, his mouth moves, over my hipbone, until he gets to my panties. He removes himself from me completely. He settles between my parted knees and hooks his fingers into the waistband. His green eyes lock on mine.

I bite my lower lip and nod, telling him to take them. That silent action is all he needs. He tugs them down my thighs, exposing me to him.

I feel my face blush, and I smile from embarrassment. I've been with my share of guys, but they've never been like this. They've all taken what they wanted like it was a race. Damon, he's teasing and memorizing, savoring. His hands land on my thighs, and he uses his thumbs to separate my folds. His lips turn up at the corners as his thumb grazes over my hard nub. My hips buck upward.

"You're so beautiful, Jazmine. Every fucking part of you." He slides a finger inside me, and I let out a whimper. With my eyes closed, I don't know that's he's lowering his mouth to me until he sucks my clit into his mouth. My eyes pop open at the same time my hips leap upward.

"Damon," I call out, voice shaking. "I've never..."

He pulls away, looks me in the eye, and smiles. "Good. At least I get one of your firsts," he says, lowering his mouth back to me.

My eyes close again, and it feels like I'm spinning out of control. Every muscle tightens while he flicks his tongue against my clit over and over. When he slides his finger into me, I break, and my orgasm floods over my entire body. My fingers lace into his hair, pulling while my hips grind into his face. I'm moaning, panting, and crying his name again and again until every muscle feels weak and drained. I don't even realize when he pulls away. I'm too lost in this feeling—the feeling of the best orgasm of my life.

"How was it?" he asks, taking his place on top of me.

I smile and hum. "Oh my god, Damon," I say around a soft giggle.

"That's not even the best part." He reaches over and opens the top drawer of his bedside table. He pulls out a shiny, silver package.

I'm feeling overwhelmed. Happy and excited but also nervous. I pull his mouth to mine and kiss him deeply while he lifts his hips and slides on the condom. Lowing his hips, he breaks the kiss.

"Are you sure, Jazmine?"

"I've always been sure about you, Damon," I whisper.

His mouth smashes against mine, and he guides himself into me.

The moment we connect, it's like fireworks going off. Everything feels right in the world. We're one.

He rocks his hips against me, teasing that perfect spot inside of me.

"Fuck, you were made for me, Jazmine," he whispers.

With his breath tickling my cheek and his hard cock teasing that spot, my muscles tighten, and he lets out a deep moan. "Fuck, you feel too good. So perfect."

"I want to ride you, Damon," I admit softly into his ear while digging my nails into his back. He quickly rolls us over so I'm on top and our eyes lock. I place my hands on his chest and begin to move up and down his length. His hands land on my hips, squeezing and pulling me down into his thrusts. I rock my hips against his and he makes a humming sound deep in his chest as his eyes flutter closed. My head dips back as my release builds. My lips part and my heavy breathing escapes. I can feel my muscles convulsing around his thick cock, and just as my high peaks, he thrusts upward, pushing me over the edge. He holds me close to his chest while moving inside of me, not releasing me until I've ridden out every last wave.

10

DAMON

I'm almost afraid to open my eyes. I feel like last night was a dream, and if I keep my eyes closed, she will always be here next to me. But if I open them, she could be gone. I feel her warm breath on my shoulder, and I turn my head and open my eyes. The sun streaming through the window is bright, but I strain against it to see her at my side. She's completely naked from last night, and she's laying on her stomach, uncovered, as she clutches a pillow beneath her chest. Her blonde hair is splayed out across my pillows, and her lips are in a pout. She's breathtaking. The smallest of whimpers leaves her lips, and I can't control myself. I roll to my side and press a soft kiss to her shoulder.

The corners of her lips turn up only slightly, but I take this as a sign to keep going. I move my lips over just an inch and press another kiss to her soft, warm skin. She stretches her neck, giving me more room to continue. I find myself between her legs, peppering her neck and back with kisses. She lifts her ass in the air, and immediately, my hands start massaging and kneading.

She takes a deep breath. "Damon, I need to feel you," she says in a whisper, lifting her hips off the bed once again. I slide my finger inside her, and she sucks in a loud breath. With the position we're in,

I can see everything, and before I know it, I'm barely holding it together. The next time she lifts her hips into the air, I take myself in hand and slide inside. This gets an automatic moan from both of us. I've never had sex without a condom before. She's too warm, wet, and tight around me. I only thrust into her a couple of times before I'm pulling out to get a condom. Leaning over the bed to reach for the drawer, her hand catches mine, and our eyes meet.

"Just a little longer? I want to feel you with nothing between us. I'm clean and on the pill. I trust you."

I swallow down my fear. "I won't last long, Jazmine. You're too perfect—feel too good."

She doesn't argue, but I can tell by the way her eyes fall to the bed that she's disappointed, so instead of continuing with my plan of the condom, I move back into position so we can become one, with nothing between us.

The second we connect, I go blind. I can't see anything. All I can do is revel in this magical feeling. I'm lost to her cries and gasps, to the way she wiggles her ass against my hips, to her heat.

I feel her muscles start to twitch around me. It's like she's milking my dick for every last drop. My release is also rising, and I don't know if I can hold out long enough for her to get what she needs.

"I'm almost there, Jazmine. Help me. Push yourself over the edge." I pick up her hand and place it against her clit. While I pump inside her, her hand works her clit until every muscle tightens and she's crying beneath me. Finally, I pull out and take myself in hand, working up and down my length until I spill myself onto her ass and lower back.

With my chest heaving, I fall to her side and grab a tissue off the table. I quickly clean her up and then pull her to my chest. I can feel her heart racing right alongside mine, her breathing just as erratic.

"You were made for me, Jazmine. Everything about you is exactly what I need," I whisper into her hair.

I hold her and watch her drift back off to sleep. It's weird. I've never done this with any other woman. I mean, I've slept with many, but I never was big into the whole cuddling thing. Laying here with

Jazz, it makes me feel as if I have a purpose. Like I'm supposed to be here, holding her, protecting her, loving her.

I hold her until I can't anymore. I slide my arm out from under her and rush to the bathroom. After relieving myself, I turn on the shower and step beneath the hot flow of water. Closing my eyes, I see nothing but the memories from last night: her soft, sun-kissed skin, her blonde hair spread across my pillows, her thick, parted lips. I can hear her whimpers, moans, and cries. I hear my name falling from her lips with more passion than I've ever experienced. There's always been something about her I couldn't turn away from. But now, that hold she has on me has only gotten tighter.

After washing off, I step out and wrap a towel around my hips. I walk back into the bedroom in time to see her roll over and stretch.

"Good morning, beautiful," I whisper against her lips when I lean over her for a kiss.

She gives me a sleepy smile. "Morning."

I pull away and move to the closet for some clothes.

"Did you shower without me?" she asks, sitting up and letting the blanket fall from her chest.

"I did, but there's plenty of hot water left. Why don't you go get cleaned up and I'll start on some breakfast?" I step out of the closet, tugging a shirt over my head.

"I'm starving," she mumbles, standing up.

I have to swallow down my desire. "I figured. You've always had an appetite."

She gives me a half smile before gliding past me, into the bathroom.

I walk through the house and into the kitchen. I pour a glass of orange juice and dig around for the needed ingredients. After finding everything I need, I turn on the waffle iron and start a pot of coffee.

By the time she's stepping out of the shower, the table is set with coffee, fresh waffles with all the toppings, bacon, and scrambled eggs.

"Something smells amazing," she says, wrapping her arms around my waist from behind.

I spin in her arms and pull her in for a kiss. "I remembered that sweet tooth of yours and decided waffles were the way to go."

She smiles. "Thank you."

I press a quick kiss to her lips. "Sit down and eat."

She releases me and sits at the table. "I hope you don't mind, but I borrowed a pair of your basketball shorts and this t-shirt. I didn't have anything but that dress."

I sit across from her. "I don't mind at all. Even though I have to admit, I'd rather keep you naked."

She laughs and rolls her eyes as she picks up a piece of bacon and takes a bite.

We're just finishing with breakfast when her phone rings.

"Where is it?" she asks, running toward the front door. We both stop to see our mess of clothes we left on the floor. We both freeze for a split second, remembering. Finally, she kicks her dress out of the way and finds her small purse. She drops to her knees and opens it, pulling out the phone.

"Hello?" she answers. "Hey, Maddie. What's up?"

My eyes grow wide as I leave her alone to talk while I go clean up the breakfast mess. I get everything loaded into the dishwasher and walk out of the kitchen to find her sitting on the couch, still talking on the phone.

I sit down at her feet, on the far end of the couch.

"Ugh, no I'm not home, and I'm sorry I didn't let you know. I got really sick last night, and Damon was afraid to leave me alone. So, he brought me back to his place. I admit, it's not bad watching him wait on me hand and foot," she giggles. "Yeah, I'll be home later. I think I'm going to take a quick nap first and let all this food settle."

I pick up her ankle and press a kiss to the inside.

Her dark eyes light up, and she smiles.

"Okay, love you too." Without another word, she hangs up the phone.

"What was that about?"

"Maddie just wanted to make sure I was safe and sound."

I scoff. "Like I haven't taken care of you nearly every day of your life. You'd think she'd trust me by now."

"She's a little confused, I think."

"About?" I ask, massaging her foot.

"Us. I think she's picking up on the little things."

"Well then, we better have as much fun as we can before she figures it out." I lift one of her legs over my head and lay down between her knees. She pulls my head to her chest, running her fingers through my hair, instantly relaxing me.

"Damon?"

"Hmm?" I ask, peaking one eye open.

"Tell me about Martin Gregs."

I lift my head to look into her eyes. "What about him?"

"I remember he got beat up on prom night. But I also remember you taking me home and staying with me until I fell asleep. If you were with me, how'd you beat him up?"

"Once you fell asleep, I left and went back to the party. I found him in a bedroom. He was with another girl, and she was passed out. She was stripped down to her underwear. You were lucky I found you when I did."

"I know. And thank you."

"For what?" I ask.

"For always being there. I think I took you for granted a lot of the time. It was never a question of if you'd be there. It was when. I knew you'd always do everything you could to rescue me."

"You don't have to thank me, Jazz. It's what I do. I told you, you've always been mine."

She lets out a soft laugh. "I wish I knew that sooner. You don't know how many girls I was jealous of in high school. I wished I was as tall as that one, or that my boobs were as big as this other one. I never thought you looked at me in any way other than a little sister."

I take a deep breath. "That's one of my biggest regrets. I wish I would've known myself sooner. If I had, we would've been together long ago."

"I think it worked out the way it was supposed to. Someone told me that we had to date all the wrong people in order to appreciate the right one."

I smile up at her, knowing those are words I said to her, even though she doesn't know that. "Who said that?"

She shrugs. "I read it somewhere."

———

WE END up laying on the couch all day, cuddling, talking, and kissing. We eat, drink, and watch tv. We order pizza for dinner and then head to the bedroom. We both get into the shower, and I can't help but watch as she steps below the hot flow of water. It cascades down her blonde hair, over her chest, and down her flat, toned stomach. I reach out and pour some shampoo into my hand, and then massage it into her hair. She keeps her head back and eyes closed, just enjoying my touch.

"What are you going to tell Maddie?" I ask, remembering how she told her she would be home later.

She shrugs. "I doubt I have to tell her anything. She was still with Travis when she called. If I know her, they've spent their day in bed."

I make a fake gagging sound. "Not what I want to hear about my little sister. And that Travis guy is up to no good."

"What? Why would you say that?"

I rinse the shampoo from her hair and start adding conditioner. "Did you see the same guy I did? He was covered in tattoos. I mean, what kind of job can he get looking like that?"

"Model?" she jokes.

"Ha ha." I rinse the conditioner from her hair. "I hope she isn't thinking about getting serious with this guy. Do you know anything about him?"

She steps out of the water so I can move into it to wash my hair.

"All I know is she's been on four dates with him, and he works for some start-up company. I highly doubt she gets serious. I hate to say it, but you and your sister are more alike than you think."

"What's that supposed to mean?"

"You both bounce around from one person to the next."

I shake my head. "Nope, I'm done with that. You're my last bounce," I joke.

"You better say that." She steps up to me and presses her lips to mine.

I pull her closer, pick her up against me, and carry her to bed, dripping wet.

I WAKE up on Sunday and have coffee and muffins made before Jazz even wakes up. I have a whole day planned. Yesterday, we spent the day lounging around and making love, but today, we're getting out of the house—going out in public, so it doesn't feel like we have to hide something so great.

After we eat, we swing by her place so she can get on something a little more comfortable.

"Where are we going?" she asks from her bedroom.

I'm sitting on her couch in the living room because I knew that if I watched her change, we'd never leave her bed. "It's a surprise."

"Well, how am I supposed to know what to wear?" She walks into the living room in only a bra and panties.

"Wear something comfortable."

"Like going to the gym comfortable or going to lunch comfortable?"

I laugh and roll my eyes. "Just put on some jeans, shoes, and a shirt."

She rolls her eyes but doesn't say anything as she goes to get dressed.

As I wait, I find a photo album on the coffee table. I lean forward and pick it up, flipping through it. I smile when I see a picture the three of us took on Halloween one year. I'm dressed as Superman, Maddie is Wonder Woman, and Jazz is The Flash. She never was into stereotypes. It didn't matter to her that The Flash was a guy. She just wanted to be the fastest there was. I remember we used to always race, and I'd beat her every time. But that day, when she was dressed as The Flash, I let her win. She beat me to every door. I was so happy to see her laugh—even if she did make fun of me for being a loser. The next day, everything went back to normal—she couldn't beat me, but for that night, she felt like she had it all.

"Whatcha lookin' at?" she asks, stepping back into the room.

"Halloween pictures."

She looks down at the picture and smiles. "I remember that. You were so sweet that night. You let me win all the races because I was The Flash." She takes the book and sits down on my lap. "For a mean-ass boy, you had your moments."

I laugh. "And for a mean-ass girl, you had yours too—like that time I lost my brand-new Batman lunchbox. You spent all afternoon helping me look for it." I shake my head. "I can't believe we never found that. You know how much that thing would be worth now?"

"How much?"

I roll my eyes. "I have no idea actually, but it was a collector's item back then. My dad was pissed when he found out I defied him and lost it. I wasn't supposed to take it out of the house. I wasn't supposed to touch it, to be honest."

She stands up. "I'll be right back."

A second later, she's standing in front of me with something behind her back.

"Please don't hate me," she says, showing me my lunch box.

11

JAZMINE

"That's my lunchbox!" Damon says, bolting upright and yanking it from my hands.

I nod my head. "I know. I found it in the weeds the next day. I guess it fell off the back of your bike when we left the secret clubhouse you built out in the woods."

"Why didn't you tell me?" he asks, opening it up and finding the matching thermos.

I shrug. "I don't know. I guess, I just wanted to have a piece of you with me, a piece that you loved so much."

"You've had this the whole time?"

I nod. "Are you mad?" I ask, scrunching my nose and shying away.

He laughs. "No way! I'm excited. Honestly, if I'd had it, it would've been torn up by now. Thank you." He pulls me into him, pressing his lips to mine. My eyes close and I live in this kiss, all our kisses. I never in a million years thought we'd be this close or that I'd ever get what I always wanted.

"You're welcome," I whisper against his lips as I lace my finger through his thick, dark hair.

"Are you ready to get on with our day?" he asks, resting his forehead against mine.

I nod. "Let's do it."

I lock up the apartment behind us, and he leads me back down to his Jeep. We stop and fill up with gas, grab a soda and some snacks, and hit the road. The drive isn't long, only about an hour with heavy lunchtime traffic. And I don't realize where we're going until he pulls into our old neighborhood.

Back when we were kids, both our families lived outside the city. Back then, nobody wanted to raise kids in Chicago, so most families lived just outside city limits—close enough they could drive to their jobs in the city while their kids still had the country life and small schools.

He turns onto our street and into his old driveway. Both of our old houses have been redone now and look nothing like the way they used to.

"My parents still own this house. They've been renting it out for years," he says, opening his door and climbing out. He comes around and opens mine, and I step out.

"About a month ago, my mom told me that the tenants had moved. When I found out the other day that it was still empty, I thought this would be a good time to come back and relive old memories. What do you think?"

"We get to go in?" I ask, wide-eyed and happy about taking a walk down memory lane.

"If you want."

I smile and nod as he takes my hand and pulls me around the Jeep, toward the door.

"Wait!" I stop walking, and he freezes, looking back at me.

"Stand right here." I take him by his shoulder and move him in front of me.

He smiles. "I was standing right here when you came walking up in that sexy as fuck punk rocker costume."

I smile and nod.

Slowly, he walks a circle around me, the same way he did all those years ago. "You're just as beautiful now as you were all those years ago," he says, coming to a stop in front of me again, but this time, he leans in and kisses me deeply. When he pulls away, he says, "That's what I should have done the first time."

I smile. "So not only are we reliving old memories, but we're rewriting them?"

"Why not? I'm not going to do it wrong a second time."

"Oh, my God. Is that you, Damon?" a woman shouts, walking over from across the street.

I turn to face her, wrapping my hand around his elbow. "Who is that?"

"I think it's Mrs. Weaver," he whispers.

"Well, it is you. How have you been, hun?" she asks, pulling him in for a hug and causing me to release him.

This lady has to be pushing sixty by now, but she looks the same as she did when we were growing up. I remember Damon had the biggest crush on her. He'd always tease her son by telling him what a MILF his mom was.

"I'm good, Mrs. Weaver. How are you?"

She smiles and pulls away, "I'm wonderful. And are you the girl from next door?"

I force a smile onto my face and nod. "I'm Jazmine."

"That's right. Please excuse me for forgetting your name, but it's been a long time. I never forget a face, though."

"It's quite alright," I assure her.

She turns her attention back to Damon. "What in the world are you doing back here after all these years?"

"Mom told me she hadn't found anyone to rent this place out to yet, and I thought it'd be a good idea to come check it out." Damon puts his arm around my shoulders and pulls me into his side.

Her eyes glance from him to me and back with a big smile. "Are you two finally together? I always knew you'd end up with one another. I remember watching this little girl pine over you," she says, looking at Damon.

I laugh, and he smiles. "I finally smartened up. I don't know why it took me so long. Look, Mrs. Weaver, we're kind of pressed for time, and we'd like to go inside and look around," Damon says, trying to cut the reunion short.

"I completely understand, dear. You two have fun and come back and visit from time to time. I think I'm the only one left in the neighborhood. Everyone that lives here now is all new with little ones of their own."

"Will do, Mrs. Weaver," Damon says, waving her off.

We stand and watch her walk back across the street before turning around and heading for the door.

"She's the lady you had a crush on, right?"

He laughs, dipping his head back. "She is," he replies, sliding the key into the lock.

"And?"

"And what?" he asks, studying me.

"How's the fantasy holding up? Does she look as good as you remember?" I'm grinning from ear to ear, enjoying teasing him.

He shakes his head. "I admit, she still looks pretty good for her age, but I've got something better now." He pulls me against him, pressing his lips to mine as he walks us into the house.

He spins me around and sets me on my feet, breaking the kiss. "Are you ready for memory lane?" He steps out of my way, and I can see the foyer I used to run in every day. It's dark, since there are no windows, but enough light shines in from the other rooms that it's easy to see. The cream carpet has been ripped up and replaced with linoleum, and the gray walls are now an off-white color.

I laugh. "Oh my gosh. I still remember there being a table here that your mom always set her purse and keys down on." I point at the wall where the table used to set.

He laughs and nods. "Let's see the rest." He takes my hand and leads me into the living room. This room has been redone as well, but it's easy to see how it used to be. Next are the dining room and kitchen. The kitchen island is still here, and I sit where I always did. He moves to the other side.

"Now all we need is a cereal box," I joke.

"I'd rather see your face than the back of a cereal box. I guess that hasn't changed."

I smile. I love hearing about how he used to feel about me because to me, it's all new. I never knew how he felt. I always felt so alone.

"Ready to go upstairs?" He winks at me.

I hop up and he leads me up the stairs, stopping in his old room first. As soon as the door opens, it's like a time warp. I'm not seeing the room how it is now. I'm seeing it how it used to be. I can see his full-sized bed shoved into the corner of the room. The nightstand with a single drawer—that's where Maddie and I found all his old Playboy magazines. His desk that was always covered in computer gaming equipment, and his dresser that held his hair gel, deodorant, and cologne. I can still see the posters he had on the walls of famous models and basketball stars. I smile just being back here.

"What do you think?"

I sit on the floor and lean back, right where his bed used to be. Smiling, I say, "I can't believe I'm in your room." I sit up and put my finger against my lips. "Shhh, if your sister finds out, she'll tell your mom for sure."

He laughs and sits down on the floor next to me. "I wish I would've brought you in here then."

"Well, let's rewrite that." I move until I'm straddling him. He reaches up and pushes my blonde hair behind my ears.

"You're so beautiful. Always have been. When I was eighteen and getting ready to leave for college, I laid here and thought about getting you in my bed. I wanted to be the one that took that virginity of yours." He kisses me softly, and it sets my body on fire. "That's why I was all over you two when guys were involved. I wasn't trying to protect you. I was only trying to save you for myself."

I reach up and run my hands through his thick brown hair. "There was this one time when I had just turned sixteen that I stayed the night with Maddie. Your parents had gone out and me and Maddie snuck in a bottle of Vodka. She got hammered and passed out. I was laying there, almost asleep. But then I heard your truck pull into the drive, and I got up on my knees and looked out the window to see you opening the passenger side door for this blonde girl. She stepped out and you pinned her to the side of your truck, kissing her and touching her. I was so angry with you, but I admit, watching that made me hot. I was still a virgin then. I hadn't done anything but kiss a few random guys, but watching you with her, I knew what I wanted."

I swallow down the fear that thinking about this next part brings on. "You brought her up to your room, and Maddie's closet is on the other side of the wall your bed is on. I crawled into her closet and put my ear to the wall. I listened while you two had sex. And even though I was pissed because I wanted to be her, your grunts and moans made me sweat. It made my blood boil beneath my skin. When the bed started banging off the wall, I couldn't listen anymore. I leaned my head back, closed my eyes, and imagined hearing my name fall from your lips. I imagined it was me making you make those noises, and I touched myself for the first time."

My face burns with embarrassment. I've never in my life admitted that to anyone.

He raises his hand and runs his thumb across my cheek. "I remember that night. That was the night I caught you making out with Jake Willard in the hot tub."

My mouth drops open. I didn't know he knew about that.

"After my parents left, I went outside to tell you guys I was leaving, and you and Jake were all alone in the dark. You were sitting on him and kissing him. Your bathing suit top was off, and he was touching you in ways I wanted to touch you. I got so pissed off, I didn't even say anything. I just turned around and left. I went to a party, and I was in a shit mood. I thought you were going to have sex with him. I thought I'd lost my chance. That's why I brought that blonde girl home. She was the closest I could get to you." He clears his throat. "The whole time I was with her, I was pretending she was you. I think I even called her Jazmine once."

I giggle. "I can't believe this. If we'd just been honest with one another back then, we wouldn't have had to wait so long."

He rolls over, putting me underneath him. "How about we rewrite this memory? Instead of being in here with that girl, I'm here with you. Instead of you making out with Jake, you're here with me. Maddie's gone to a party, and my parents are nowhere to be found."

I smile. "I like the sound of that," I say, pulling his lips to mine.

Even though we're still clothed, he grinds his hips into mine, and I let out a gasp. That sound only makes him thrust against me while his hand massages my breast. He breaks our kiss and lowers his mouth to my stomach, kissing his way up, pushing my shirt up as he goes. I reach for it and pull it off, dropping it beside me. He doesn't even bother with unhooking my bra. Instead, he pulls the cups down, letting them spill over. He has a hand on each of them, kissing, sucking, and nibbling. My mouth opens, and I call out his name.

"Damon." It comes out in a soft whisper.

His hands fall to the button on my jeans and he quickly unfastens them and slides them down my legs. While he's still up on his knees, he pulls his jeans down past his hips. His toned six-pack is on full display when he reaches behind him and pulls off his shirt.

I reach for him, and he comes without me having to ask. He settles himself between my parted knees, guiding his cock between my folds.

"I don't have a condom," he whispers in a deep voice. A voice that I now know he only has when he's turned on.

"I don't care. I need this memory."

He smirks just as he pushes forward, entering me. He feels so good that my eyes want to close the instant we become one, but I force them to stay open, to stay locked with his darkening green eyes. I watch as his brows pull together with the overwhelming pleasure. He bites his lower lip as he moves in and out of me. His chest, arms, and stomach flex with his every thrust. Watching him while having this connection makes my release rise. My muscles begin to harden, and my breathing picks up.

"Damon, I'm going to come," I call out, not pulling my eyes from his.

"Fuck, me too, Jazmine." He starts pumping harder and faster, pushing both of us over the edge. Just as my release ends, he pulls out and uses his hand to empty himself onto my stomach.

He lets out a deep breath and wipes the sweat from his forehead. "Fuck, I'm sorry. I didn't know what else to do." He begins looking around for something to clean up with.

"Look in the bathroom. See if a roll of toilet paper got left behind."

He stands, pulls his jeans back up over his hips, and walks into the hall. He's back within seconds with a wad of toilet paper. He kneels down and wipes my stomach clean, then collapses at my side, pulling me against him and pressing a kiss to my shoulder.

12

DAMON

Being with her, here in my childhood home, it makes it feel like everything has come full circle. I can't count how many times I laid in this room, dreaming about being with her in every way possible. To be honest, at the time, I was a horny teenager and only wanted one thing. She was the sexiest girl I'd ever seen. She had the body of a woman while being the girl next door. Every year I waited for summer, just so I could see her long, tan legs, round ass, flat stomach, and the most perfect tits. The sad part was I hadn't even seen them at the time, not without something in the way like a bikini top.

I once had a party after graduation, and she showed up in a white t-shirt. I could tell automatically that she wasn't wearing a bra. So what did I do? I got her alone and then accidentally poured my beer on her. I wasn't trying to see her tits. I was trying to keep everyone else from seeing her tits. But, in the process, I got the full view. Her shirt clung to her chest, and it showed everything: the swell of her breast, her hard, pink nipples. She screamed at me of course and covered herself before running up to Maddie's room to change, but fuck. I had good material to jack off to later that night.

I let out a deep chuckle, and she studies my face. "What's so funny?"

"I was just thinking about that party you came to. The one where I poured beer on you to make you go change."

She laughs. "You mean the one where you totally got to see my boobs?"

I nod. "That's the one. To be fair, I wasn't trying to see your boobs. I just didn't want anyone else to either and a white shirt with no bra? What in the hell were you thinking?"

Her face reddens. "I was trying to get your attention."

"You've always had my attention, Jazz. Always." I get myself up to my knees and pull her up with me. "And, I ended up missing the party so I could hide out in my room and jerk off."

She laughs loud and smacks my bare chest. "You did not!"

"I swear," I say, fixing her bra. "If you'd had let me, I would've licked every bit of beer off your chest."

"Hey, do you remember that time we played spin the bottle?" she asks, pulling her shirt back on.

I roll my eyes. "How could I forget it?"

I grab the case of soda and take it to the basement for the 'study group' Mom said I could have tonight. Little does she know, it's not a study group. It's just a random get-together. There are six guys, including me, and only four girls. Matt comes walking in from the outside door.

"Hey, I found two more girls."

I look up to see my sister and Jazz. "They're only fourteen. No way are they playing spin the bottle."

"Come on, man, if you land on your sister, we'll let ya spin again. And it's not like it's going to be anything serious. It's just spin the bottle."

"She's not having her first kiss with one of you assholes," I say, setting down the soda.

"For your information, I've already had my first kiss," Maddie states matter-of-factly.

I roll my eyes and scoff, not believing her. "Whatever. I'm sick of arguing with you guys."

We all sit in a circle, and Matt spins first. We all watch that bottle go around and around before stopping on Jessica. I can see the excitement on his face. Everyone knows he has a thing for her and is too chicken to ask her out. They both get up on their knees and lean in for the kiss. He plans on just giving her a quick peck, but she holds on to his face, and he can't get away.

Everyone in the group catcalls them, cheering them on. Finally, they break apart. But they don't stick around either. Being seventeen, all we can think about is making out and getting lucky. The whole point of playing this game was to get everyone to loosen up to have a make-out party.

I spin the bottle next and hold my breath until it stops spinning. I look at the bottle and follow it up to the person it's pointing to. Jazmine.

Fuck. Not that Jazmine is a total dog or anything, but she's only four-teen. I can't make out with her all night. I take a deep breath and get up to my knees. She does the same. We both lean forward, and our lips touch. I hold my mouth against hers for what seems like a few seconds, then pull away. Her cheeks are red, but she remains cool as she sits back down. My heart is pounding uncontrollably, but I take my seat and pass the bottle for the next person's turn. The rest of the night, I can't keep my eyes off her.

"You were my first kiss," she says, standing and sliding her jeans back on.

I smile. "I was?"

She nods. "And Jeremy was Maddie's first kiss."

I laugh. "And she made such a big deal about having kissed someone before."

She laughs. "We wanted to be cool too. No way was I going to admit in a room full of seventeen-year-olds that I hadn't kissed anyone. Maddie was the same way."

I laugh and shake my head. "You two were always a handful." I look at my watch and see that it's going on noon. "Come on. I have more plans for us."

She smiles, slides on her shoes, and follows along behind me. I lead her out of the house and lock it up behind us, walk around to the back of the Jeep, and take out the picnic basket and cooler I'd packed this morning.

"Are we having a picnic?" she asks with glistening eyes and a smile.

I nod. "Yep, follow me." I head toward the backyard. Just past the property line is the forest. We used to play back here all the time. I even built our clubhouse out here when we were little. I haven't been back here in years. I have no idea if it's even still standing. But if it's not, that's okay too.

She gasps from behind me. "Oh my god. We're going to the clubhouse, aren't we?"

"We're going to try. I hope a storm hasn't knocked it down. I mean, it was a group of eight-year-olds that built it."

She laughs. "I walked out here before college and it was still standing. It was not in the best shape, but it was still there."

"Really? Why'd you do that?"

She shrugs. "I was missing you. I couldn't just walk into your room with your sister and parents. This was the next best place."

I hold out my hand and she takes it. "I wish things had been different."

"That's a wish we both have," she says, breathless.

"Yeah, but I think things were different for us. I was a dumbass teenager. I was pining for you but too damn stubborn to admit it. Instead of being honest with myself and you, I tried to pretend it didn't exist and ended up using a lot of girls to try and make up for not having you."

She rolls her eyes. "You didn't mind. And I'm sure those girls didn't either."

"I did mind. I hated myself because I knew deep down, I wanted you but was too afraid to do anything about it. I was afraid you'd turn me down, or my sister or our parents would have a problem with it. I knew I'd be leaving for college, and even though I was in love with you, wanted to have the whole college experience and didn't want to be held back." I stop and take a deep breath. "I knew I'd have you one day. I just told myself to be patient and wait until the time was right."

She grins. "And you finally decided the time was right?"

"No, but I couldn't hold back any longer." I laugh. "It took every bit of self-restraint I had back then to stop myself from taking you. I knew I couldn't do that again." I press a kiss to her hand before pulling her along a little further.

It's not too much longer before we're pushing through the break in the trees. Looking around, I find my clubhouse still up in the tree, falling apart, but it's still there. I can still see the sign on the front that reads, "no girls" and then the place under it that says, "except Maddie and Jazz" that they added on when I wasn't around. On the ground below the tree is the fire pit, and surrounding it are all the big rocks and boulders we pulled back in with the wagon.

"I can't believe all this is still here," I say, setting the cooler down next to the grown-up fire pit.

"I told you. I wonder how come no neighborhood kids have found it and claimed it as their own?"

"Probably because kids don't play outside anymore. That and when they do, their parents won't let them out of their sight. The world is a different place than what we grew up in."

She shrugs. "I guess you're right." She sits down on a rock. "So, what did you bring for us to eat?"

I smile and open the basket. "Well, I made peanut butter and jelly sandwiches, just like we used to bring back here. There are some Goldfish crackers, and I even brought juice boxes. But I also brought a couple of beers." I laugh. "I'm a kid at heart, but I'm still an adult."

I pull out the food, and we sit and eat while looking around our old stomping ground.

"I remember when you fell out of that treehouse and ended up with five stitches in your chin," she says with a laugh.

"I remember when you tripped and fell, slicing your knee open, and I had to carry you all the way home."

"I still have a scar from that." She pulls up her jeans and shows me the tiny white scar on her knee.

When we finish our lunch, I open the cooler and pull us both out a beer. She gives me a sidelong look.

"You know I don't drink beer."

"Just take it. This is another memory I want to recreate."

She frowns but takes the beer. I pull out my phone and start up Hate That I Love You by Rihanna.

Instantly, her eyes light up, remembering the moment.

The sun has just gone down, and the forest around us is dark, only lit up by the fire raging on. Everyone is out here, the only place I could think of to have a party where we wouldn't get caught. I tried keeping Maddie and Jazz out of it, but as always, they snooped until they found out, and now I can't get them to leave. They're both standing by the tree that holds my old tree house; both have a beer in their hands. I've been watching them like a hawk and haven't seen either of them take a drink.

I'm clear across the opening, standing with a group of friends, not listening to anything they have to say. I'm too zoned out of their conversation. I'm too lost in the way Jazmine looks tonight. She's wearing a pair of cut-off jean shorts, and a white tank top with a hot pink bra underneath. Her blonde hair is ironed straight—I prefer the soft natural curl it has, but she still looks beautiful. She has way too much makeup for a girl her age, and it pisses me off that I keep my distance from her because she's so young, but all these guys keep hitting on her. I've watched her turn down more than I can count already.

The song that was playing ends and Hate That I Love You by Rihanna and Ne-Yo comes on. Our eyes lock in the darkness. She tilts her head to the side and runs her tongue across her bottom lip. Immediately, I lick my own, like I'm preparing for a kiss. Something about her eyes looks sad, and I want to go over there and check on her, but then the girl I've been fooling around with comes up to my side and says something I don't hear. And she said it plenty loud enough; I'm just too focused on Jazmine to notice.

Since I didn't hear what she said, I don't reply. I just put my arm around her and pull her to my side. When Jazz sees this, she says something to Maddie and nods back toward the house. They both toss down their beers and take off without saying a word.

With the song playing, she stands and walks over to the tree, leaning against the same way she did back then. Somehow, she even gets that sad look on her face. When our eyes lock, instead of standing in one place, I walk over to her. I pause for a split second and then grab her, pulling her in for a kiss. She tosses her beer, just like she did all those years ago, but this time, it isn't to walk away. It's to wrap her arms around my neck. I drop mine as well and then use both hands to pick her up against me. Pressing her back to the tree, I kiss her deeply and with as much passion as I can find within myself. I break the kiss and pull back enough to see her face clearly.

"Why did you have that sad look on your face that night?" I ask, brushing her blonde hair away from her face.

"I saw a flicker of something in your eyes that night when you looked at me. I thought you hated me, and it broke my heart because I loved you."

"Why would you think I hated you?"

She presses against my chest until I put her down, then walks back over to the fire pit and sits down. "I felt a connection that night when you looked at me. But it was like you were so repulsed by that connection that you hated it. And then that song on top of it. And just when I thought you were going to walk over, she came to your side, and you pulled her close. It was," she shakes her head. "It was just a stupid childish thought, I guess. For a second, I had hope, and I felt like she stole it."

I walk over to her and bend down, putting us at eye level. "I hate myself for making you feel that way. I never wanted to leave you hanging or feel like you were alone. It just..." my words break off.

"It just wasn't the right time," she finishes my sentence for me.

I crack a smile and nod. "If we'd gotten together back then, I would've fucked it up. I would've gone off to college and broken your heart. You really would hate me now. I think the universe knew that. And I think it's rooting for us. That's why it presented us with the opportunity. It's finally right. I finally have you, and I'm never letting go." I lean in and pull her in for another lip-crushing kiss. She kisses me back with just as much desire and love. My body begins to come alive again, but before I can do anything, a single raindrop falls and hits me on the top of the head. I pull back and look up just as the rest start to fall.

Jazmine screams and stands up, laughing and giggling.

"Come on. We're going to be soaked by the time we get back to the house." I grab her hand and pull her along behind me. We run through the woods in the storm, laughing the whole way.

By the time we hit the backyard, we're soaked, clothes clinging to our bodies. Her blonde hair is a wet mess hanging around her. But she's beautiful at this moment. There's nothing between us, and I finally know that she's mine—one hundred percent.

I pull her against me and kiss her, carrying her across the backyard and over to the side of the house, where I press her against it. Thunder cracks loudly overhead, and we pull apart.

"We better get out of the rain," I tell her, taking her hand and pulling her back to the Jeep.

———

WE'RE both cold and shivering when we pull up to her apartment building. I park in the parking lot and we run upstairs. The rain has only seemed to follow us all the way back home. She quickly gets the door open, and we rush inside. The second she steps in, she spins around and smashes her mouth to mine, pushing me back so the door slams shut.

Her hands are on a mission to strip off all of my wet clothes. Once I'm down to just my boxers, I work on ridding her of her clothes. Without our mouths never parting, we leave our wet clothes on the kitchen floor, and I pick her up against me, carrying her though the apartment until I find the bathroom. We pull apart long enough to start the shower and take off our underwear, then we're right back together under the stream of water. As we warm up, we kiss and touch, and tease. Her hand pumps me up and down, and I kiss my way along her neck and collar bone.

"I love you, Jazmine," I whisper. "I always have."

"I love you too, Damon," she says, pulling my mouth back to hers.

I'm about to pick her up and carry her to bed when we hear her front door slam shut. We pull apart quickly.

"I forgot to lock the door," I say, locking my eyes on hers.

"Jazz?" Maddie yells from in the kitchen.

"Shit," Jazz whispers, trying to get out of the shower.

I climb out behind her and wrap a towel around my waist as she tugs on her robe.

"Stay here. I'm going to get rid of her."

13

JAZMINE

I quickly run from the bathroom, being sure to shut the door behind me. I bump into Maddie in the kitchen.

"Whoa, what the hell, Jazz?" she asks, looking around my kitchen to find piles of wet clothes.

"Oh, ummm."

"Is someone here with you?" she asks, trying to peek around the door frame to look down the hall. Her eyes are wide, and she's wearing a smirk. "Oh, my God. There is, isn't there. You got laid! I can see it all over your face. Who is it? Do I know him? Is it that guy you said you met at work?" Again she tries to peek down the hall.

"Yes! Yes, it's the guy from work. I really need you to leave," I say, walking her backward, toward the door.

She jumps up and down. "You go, girl! Look at us! Both of us getting laid. Oh, we should double date!"

I open the door and push her out. "What? No! We're not dating. We just ran into one another yesterday and got to talking. We're just..." I shake my head. "We're just hooking up. Please, don't say anything to anyone about this. Okay?"

She smiles and nods. "Sure thing. Go get you some." She smacks me on the arm and walks away.

I close the door, lock it, then press my back against it, breathing heavily. Once I have my heart and breathing under control, I go back into the bathroom to find Damon sitting on the edge of the tub, a towel wrapped around his waist.

"Is she gone?" he asks, standing and walking up to me.

"Yes, she's gone. She thinks I'm sleeping with someone from work, but she's gone."

He places his hands on my hips and pulls me closer, pressing a kiss to my neck. "Well, technically, you didn't lie. You are sleeping with someone from work."

"I know, but we've only been seeing one another for less than a week, and I already feel like I'm hiding and keeping secrets. I hate it."

He pulls back to study my face. "Do you want to tell her?"

"No, not yet, anyway. This is too new."

"Then," he shrugs. "We'll keep doing what we have been."

"Lying?" I ask, crossing my arms and looking up at him from beneath my lashes.

"You need to stop overthinking everything, Jazz. I swear, the only time I can get that brain of yours to turn off is when I have you naked and beneath me." He smirks and tilts my head back to press a kiss to my lips.

I smile, happy that he's trying to lighten the mood. "Or on top of you."

"That's my girl," he says, green eyes growing darker by the moment.

I wrap my arms around his neck. "Help me turn my brain off, Damon," I ask in a whisper.

That's all he needs to hear. He picks me up and carries me to my room. He loses his towel somewhere along the way, and when we fall into bed, he's already got my robe wide open. His thick cock is already teasing my opening, and I can't help but move my hips up and down to allow it to slide between my slick folds.

"You're always so wet for me," he mutters, enjoying the feeling of nothing between us.

"You're always so hard for me," I reply with a grin on my lips.

"I've been hard for you for as long as I can remember."

"Tell me, when was the first time?"

He grins and licks his lips, starting the story...

"Come on, Mom. We have to get home. Jazz is coming home today. She's been gone all summer," Maddie yells from the backseat as Mom makes yet another stop.

"I know. You've told me a hundred times today. You've waited all summer, you can wait ten more minutes," Mom says, climbing out of the car to run into to pick up the cupcakes she ordered.

"What's the big rush?" I ask. "Like Mom said, you can wait ten more minutes," I say from my place in the front seat.

"Jazz was supposed to be home an hour ago!"

"Look, here she comes," I say, pointing to Mom rushing out of the shop with a big, white box in her hands.

It only takes a couple of minutes before we're pulling into the drive. The second we do, Jazz stands up from her seat on the porch step. My eyes double their size when I see how much she's grown over the summer.

Her blonde hair hangs nearly to her ass. Her chest is poking out more than it did the last time I saw her, and she has long, tan legs. She's had to of grown at least a foot this summer. I bet if I stood next to her, she'd be as tall as I am and I'm fifteen. She's only thirteen.

We all climb out of the car, and Maddie rushes in for a hug. "I missed you! I'm so glad you're home!"

Mom hugs her next. "Look at how you've grown. You're almost a full-grown lady."

Jazz, Mom, and Maddie all look at me.

"Well, don't be shy. Give the girl a hug," Mom says, looking at me.

I roll my eyes but lean in and hug her tightly. That chest that I noticed earlier is soft and squishy against mine. A smile forms as I feel a tingling sensation start in my stomach and work its way lower.

I quickly pull away when I realize what's happening. "Glad you're home, Jazz. Gotta go," I say, running into the house and straight to my room.

He tells me the story, and I remember it quite well. However, I have a different perspective on the whole situation. I had no idea he had gotten hard, or that that was even a thing at my age.

"I thought for sure you were going to say at your pool party. Do you remember that?"

He cocks his head to the side and thinks it over. "Refresh my memory." He places all of his weight on me as he watches my face.

"Come over, Jazz. My parents are gone, and Damon is throwing another party. The pool is open, and he's invited the whole school. There's even beer," Maddie says over the phone.

Hearing about this party makes me giddy. "Okay, let me throw on my new suit and I'll be over." I quickly hang up the phone and race to my room to find my new, two-piece bathing suit. It's my first string bikini, and it's hot pink. I know it will get Damon's attention. I hop in the shower and shave quickly before pulling it on. I throw on a bathing suit cover and slide my feet into a pair of flip flops before rushing out the door.

I let myself into the house and Maddie runs up to me, grabbing my wrist and pulling me out the back door. The party is in full swing. There are groups of people standing around the pool, drinking and talking, and the pool is full of Damon and his friends. Immediately, I pull my cover off and toss it down in the nearest chair. Maddie whistles as she looks me up and down.

"God, you suck. When am I going to get boobs like those?" She doesn't even try to hide the fact that she's looking at nothing but my boobs.

"Mads, you're kind of making me a little uncomfortable."

She scrunches up her face. "Well, you expect my stupid brother to drool over them, don't you? Why can't I? And it's not like I want to touch them. I just want some of my own." She crosses her arms over her chest.

I laugh. "One of these days, hopefully. And if not, just buy some. That's what I'm going to do when these babies start getting saggy. Just like my mom." I smile, proud that I at least have one aspect of my life worked out.

She snorts before sitting down in the chair I just threw my cover-up into.

"You think Damon will let us drink?"

She shrugs. "I don't see why not. As long as we don't tell on him, he'll let us do whatever we want." She smiles wide.

Her answer makes me smile too. I walk around the pool and up to the keg.

"Hey there, sexy," *some guy says, handing me a cup of foamy beer.*

I smile and bat my eyelashes. "Hey."

"I haven't seen you around. You go to school with us?" *he asks, taking a step closer to me while handing off the nozzle to a different guy.*

I nod. "I'm a freshman."

He purses his lips together. "A freshman, huh?"

"Yep." *I take a drink of the bitter beer and force myself to swallow it. I can't be choking over beer now.*

"Nope! Wrong! Back away!" *Damon says, stepping up next to me.* "This is my little sister's best friend, practically my little sister. She's off limits."

The other guy holds up the palms of his hands and goes back to his keg while Damon takes my arm and pulls me off the side.

"Why'd you do that? You're not my brother, you know." *I place one hand on my hip and stick my boobs out that much further.*

His glassy eyes fall downward and lock on my chest, causing a grin to spread across his face. "You're too young to be here getting trashed. These guys will take advantage of you."

I scoff. "I can take care of myself, Damon. What's so wrong with wanting to find a guy to make out with for a little while? It's not like I'm going to get knocked up from making out."

He bites his lower lip and his eyes look me up and down slowly. "Meet me in the garage in five minutes," *he says before walking away.*

"What? Why?" *I ask, but he doesn't turn back.* "Damon," *I whisper yell.*

I walk back over to Maddie and hand her my cup of beer. "Here, drink up. I'm going to the bathroom."

"What was that about?"

I roll my eyes. "Oh, you know your stupid brother. Always trying to protect me. I'll be back in a few. Hopefully, there isn't a long-ass line."

"There is," *she says, sipping on my beer while people watching.*

I let myself back into the house and walk down the hallway. I open the garage door and slip inside. It's dark, so I call out his name. "Damon?"

"Over here," *he says, opening the fridge that his dad keeps out here for beer.*

I follow the light, and when I step up to him, he pulls out a beer, takes a drink, and hands it to me. I take a sip.

"What's this about?"

"You said you wanted to make out. Make out with me." He says it all callous, more like he's doing it as a favor to me.

"What? no!"

"Why not? You don't think I could be any worse than the rest of them assholes out there, do ya?"

"No, I guess not. But you're Maddie's brother. You don't even like me like that."

"So, you think any of those guys out there are going to like you like that? All they want is someone to take advantage of. They'll take what they want and never call you again. You want that?"

"No," I mumble, crossing my arms over my chest from being berated.

"Well, if you want to make out, I'm the only one that's not going to do that. I'll let you practice on me."

I think it over quickly. "Alright," I breath out.

He reaches out and places his hands on my hips, pulling my nearly bare chest against his. I place my arms around his neck and wet my lips. Slowly, he leans in, pressing his mouth to mine. At first, it's like our kiss we had when we played spin the bottle, but then, I feel his tongue against my lips and I open them. I've never French kissed anyone in my life. I tell myself I need the experience. And who better to practice with than my life-long crush?

I open my mouth and wiggle my tongue with his, unsure of what I'm doing, wondering if I'm doing it wrong or bad. But then he spins us and presses my back to the cold fridge, and I suck in a loud breath. His hands come up to cradle my face, deepening the kiss. At this point, I'm gone. I've died and gone to heaven. I lift my hand and place it flat on his stomach, feeling his abs harden beneath my touch. A swirl starts in my belly like a tornado. It's warm and tingly, and it feels good. Then, the fire spreads, and it consumes me. I hook my leg up over his hip, pulling him closer. I can feel his hardness pressing against me. It excites me and gives me hope that this will go further.

The hand that's still on my hip moves lower, squeezing my thigh. Then moves back upward and around to my ass. I let out a soft moan, a noise I've never heard myself make, and he pulls away. He spins so his back is to me. And now I've been in the dark long enough that I can see a little more clearly, I can see how hard he's panting.

"What's wrong? Am I bad at it?" I ask, wiping my mouth.

He lets out a nervous chuckle. "No, the opposite, actually. You don't need any more practice." His voice is off; it sounds deep and a little stiff like he needs to clear his throat.

"What? Are you sure? Did you like it?"

I see his shoulders fall as a deep breath leaves his lips. "Jazz, trust me. You're good, okay? That was one of the best kisses of my life. But we can't talk about it or ever let it happen again, okay? You're too young for me. We could get in serious trouble if we don't go our separate ways now. I'm drunk, and I shouldn't have ever let this start to begin with." He turns to face me now, and I see his Adam's apple bob in his throat as he swallows down whatever he's feeling.

Instead of being happy and excited about our kiss, I'm sad. I hate that it's over and that he says it can never happen again. I thought for sure I could reel him in. That if he just had one taste of what I could offer, he wouldn't be able to turn me down.

Without a word, I walk past him and into the house, bumping into Maddie.

She frowns. "What were you doing out there?"

"Oh, ugh. Damon wanted help grabbing some beer from your dad's fridge."

"Oh," she shrugs. "Come on, let's go grab a cup and soak in the hot tub." She grabs my arm and pulls me back outside.

14

DAMON

"I had completely forgotten about that. I was so hammered that night. I woke up the next morning and thought I'd dreamt it. Why didn't you ever mention it?" I ask, looking into her eyes.

"You said we could never talk about it. I didn't want you to get into trouble. You had just turned eighteen, and I was barely fifteen. I mean, I had kissed a couple of guys, but not like that."

Just hearing about that memory, a memory I had always thought was a dream, it makes me ache to be inside her. It brings back everything I was feeling that night. It reminds me of how fucking turned on I was from having her mouth against mine, feeling her soft chest, and round ass. And that fucking whimper. She did it that night too. I remember that kiss broke me because *that's w*hen I realized, after all these years, I still wanted her, and would never get her.

She rolls us over and sits on top of me. Her blonde hair cascades over one shoulder, and her brown eyes shine. She bites her lower lip as she lifts her hips and slides down my length.

"I guess we're no longer using condoms?" I ask to the best of my ability.

She groans. "Oh, yeah." She lifts herself up, but I grab her hips and push her back down, causing her to let out a moan that makes my dick jump inside her.

"Don't," I practically beg. "I need to be inside you. Just you and me, that's all I need."

She smiles and begins moving herself up and down once again. When she's got all of me inside her, she rocks her hips before starting the tantalizing process all over again. I sit up and catch her nipple in my mouth, making her call out.

We spend the next two hours making love. I don't even care if I get off. I'm just happy being inside her, being with her, being hers.

Finally, I watch her fall fast asleep in my arms. I can't do anything but watch her, amazed by her beauty and the fact that after our childhood, she could still love me. I don't know how this will turn out. I don't know if my sister will find out and ruin it all. But I do know that I'll never be able to live without her again. I've had a taste, and I'm hooked, like any powerful drug. You only need it once to be done forever. I've found my forever. There's no way I could go back to the way we were. And I'd die if I ever have to watch her be with another man. Just the thought haunts me.

I just finished my final exams, ending my junior year of college. Since my dorm is already packed up, I go back and quickly load everything into my truck to go back home for the summer. I can't wait to be back in my old bedroom, partying with my old friends and catching up on what's going on with my sister and Jazz. It's been too long since I've seen them and been able to torture them.

I pull into the drive a little while later. Maddie is sitting on the steps, and I quickly glance around, finding Jazz on the curb. She's standing next to a beat-up car, talking with whoever is inside. I shut off the engine and step out. Maddie yells my name and comes running over, getting both Jazz's attention and that of the guy she's talking to. Jazz looks up at me, and a big smile stretches across her face. The guy she's talking to looks me up and down, then looks up to see Jazz's reaction. I can tell that his jealousy has taken over.

He opens the door, making her take a step back, and he climbs out, forcing her to look at him instead of me. He says something to her that I can't hear, and she agrees, nodding her head. He places his hands on her cheeks and leans in for a kiss.

I force myself to look away, not wanting to invade on their moment but also because I've only been home for two seconds. I don't want to be envious already. I give Maddie a hug and spin her around. When I set her on her feet, I can't keep my eyes from looking back over at Jazz and that guy. I figured they'd be done with their kiss by now, but it's only gone deeper. He now has her back to the side of his car. Her arms are around his neck, and he grabs her thigh with one hand, lifting it up over his hip. It's a move I've done a thousand times, and all it does it allow the guy to rub his dick against the girl. Seeing this paints my vision red.

Who the fuck is this guy and why is he touching her like that? Jazz is eighteen. She shouldn't be out here dry humping on the side of the road. He should have more respect for her. He shouldn't want me watching this. If I were him, I'd take her inside, that way, whatever happened between us, stayed between us. I wouldn't want to give another guy the fuel they'd need to steal her. But it's obvious this guy is a complete douche. This is the kind of guy I protected her from when I was here. But I'm not here anymore. I have three months. And at this moment, I'm determined to break them up. She deserves better.

When I see his hand wrap around her throat, I step forward. "Hey!" I yell.

Slowly, he pulls away from her. He looks pissed, but she looks mildly entertained. Is she going along with this to get a rise out of me?

"I think it's time for you to go," I tell him, walking closer.

He steps away. "Is that right?"

Jazz jumps into action, putting herself between us. "Just go, Chris. I'll call you later," she tries.

He looks at her, then me, and back. Finally, he nods and climbs behind the wheel.

We all stand and watch as his car gets further and further away. Then I turn back to her. "You need to get rid of that guy. He's fucking worthless."

She grins. "It's nice to see you too, Damon."

"Maddie, will you go inside. We'll be in in a sec," I tell her.

She nods and goes in, leaving Jazz and me alone.

"Guys like that will only use you and get you in trouble."

She shrugs. "I'm using him, Damon."

My eyes jump up and lock on hers.

"A girl's gotta have fun. I'll be going to college in a couple of months. It won't last." She steps back and leans against the side of my truck.

I step closer, nearing touching her chest with mine. Her breath hitches, her eyes grow wide at how close I am. "You keep fucking that guy, and there will be no college. You'll end up knocked up by the end of the summer." I turn to walk in the house.

"How do you know I'm fucking him?" she shouts from behind me.

I turn and look her up and down. "I can tell. You're different." I shake my head. "You're not the girl I left when I went back to college over spring break." Walking away from her after discovering the truth makes me hate myself. It should've been me. I know I would've treated her better. I wouldn't have used her. If it were me, we'd still be together right now, and this guy wouldn't be here. I would've pulled into the driveway and she would've been running to me, kissing me. But I'm too big of a pussy to tell her how I feel.

It's been a month since Jazz, and I have gotten together, and so far, nobody has found out. We keep our work life professional, as professional as we ever kept it, and we spend as much time together after work as we can. Of course, she still has to dodge Maddie's attempts at hooking her up with men. But luckily for us, Maddie's been preoccupied with her relationship with Travis, so she hasn't given us much attention yet. Everything seems to be going as perfectly as it can.

"Ugh, Damon, did you get the same email I did from your mom?" Jazz asks from her desk on the other side of my office.

"What? What email?" I ask, clicking around on my computer to find the email she's referring to. I read over it quickly. Mom's back from her spa trip and wants everyone to get together for our monthly dinner at her place this weekend. This is something she started doing once we were all in college and joining the workforce. All of our schedules were so different, and being younger, you don't make a lot of time for family dinners. So, she started this up and none of us have ever missed a dinner.

"Monthly dinner," I mumble.

"Yep. And we have to go. We've never missed one. If we do now, they'll know something is up," Jazz says, standing and pacing the floor.

I stand and walk up to her, stopping her in her tracks. "It's been a month. Don't you think we should let them in on our little secret?"

Her eyes flash from me to the floor and back, unsure. "I don't know, Damon. I mean, things are going so great. I'd hate to mess that up by getting our family involved. I mean, what if they think it's sick or something? I'm basically your sister." She raises her brows.

A gagging sound escapes my mouth. "Don't say that. You're not my sister, and nobody thinks of us that way. You didn't live with us. My mom didn't have to raise you. You're my sister's best friend that I happened to know growing up. It's not that bad, Jazz." I place my hands on her biceps. "Do I have to get you naked to make you stop overthinking this? Cuz' you know I will," I tease with a side grin.

She laughs and smacks my arm. "I'll think about it."

"That's all I ask." I close the space between us, landing a solid kiss to her lips.

"Your place or mine tonight?" I ask, pulling away.

She shrugs and walks back to her desk. "Whatever. Mine is closer to the office, but yours is further from your sister's," she laughs out.

"Oh, she's my sister now?" I tease, placing my hands on top of her desk and leaning down for another kiss. I know I'll never be able to get enough of this woman. She's been mine for the last month, and I still can't keep my hands off her.

I hear my office door open, and I pull away and spin around to find Maddie standing there, frozen, trying to understand what she's just seen.

"Mads," Jazz says, standing up. "It's not..." she starts, but her sentence drifts off.

"What?" she says, shutting the door. "When?" She motions between us. "How?" She finally gives up on trying to form a sentence.

I take a deep breath to clear my head. "Come on, Maddie. You had to have known what's been going on. I mean, you've known us your whole life," I state.

She shakes her head. "No, Jazz has been in love with you since we were kids. I knew that much. But when did things change for you? And why the fuck didn't anyone tell me? I mean, did you think I'd be pissed that my brother and best friend found love? You two really think that little of me?" Her blue eyes are starting to water, and her hands are clenched into fists. "Does Mom know?"

"No, we were just talking about telling everyone at dinner this weekend," Jazz says.

"Oh, isn't that convenient? I find out, and suddenly you're in a hurry to tell everyone? Wait, was that you at her apartment a month ago? When I walked in and found wet clothes all over the floor?" She looks at me, eyes narrowing.

I slide my hands into my pockets and nod once.

She scoffs. "I can't believe you two have been lying to me all this time." She shakes her head and turns to leave.

"Mads, wait!" Jazz tries, but she marches out and slams the door behind her.

Slowly, I turn and look at Jazmine. She's glaring back at me, but I know she isn't angry with me. She's angry at the whole situation.

"Just let her go and cool off. You can call her later and explain everything."

"How am I supposed to explain it, Damon? Sorry, but I didn't trust you to not ruin this for me?"

I wave her off. "That's not it and you know it. Just explain it to her like you'd explain it to me. It was new and different. We didn't know if it'd even last. We didn't want pressure from the family... All that stuff."

She hangs her head, and I walk around her desk, dropping to my knees. She spins her chair in my direction, and she hugs me close. "I'm sorry. I didn't mean to snap at you. I'm just stressed and worried that I may have screwed up the only relationship I've had since I was five-years-old."

"Shh, you don't have to be sorry. I'm here for you. If it's your fight, it's my fight."

WHEN THE WORKDAY ENDS, we pack up and head out. I place my arm around her shoulder and lead her to my Jeep in the parking lot.

"So, your place or mine?" I ask, climbing behind the wheel.

"Actually, can you just take me home? I need to get ahold of Maddie and explain."

I nod once. "Sure." I start the vehicle and look back over at her. "Do you want me to come with you?"

She shakes her head. "I think it will be easier if it came from me. All those years with our stolen touches and kisses, I never told her about any of it. So, I'm sure all this seems sudden to her. I want to tell her everything."

"Everything?"

"Everything."

"Okay. If that's what you want." I shift into drive and go directly to her place. Pulling up out front, I put the car in park. "Do you want to grab dinner or anything first? I know you don't have anything in that apartment of yours to eat."

She gives me a weak smile. "Thank you." She leans in and presses a soft kiss to my lips.

"For what?"

"For everything. For caring about me even when I thought you didn't, for watching out for me above all else, for being a friend, a love, family. All of it."

"Jazmine?" I whisper, not sure of why she's saying these things. I reach over and cup her cheeks, looking deeply in her eyes for anything she may be holding back.

"I'm fine. We're fine." She gives me one last kiss and pulls away. "I'll call you later, okay?"

"Okay," I agree, watching her go.

I sit behind the wheel and watch her until she steps into the building safely. When I'm sure she's not stepping back out, I shift into drive and head home.

Walking into my house feels weird. This past month, I've had her with me every day. We'd come home from work, to her place or mine, we'd have dinner together, cuddle on the couch and watch tv, we'd shower, and head to bed for more cuddling, talking, or lovemaking. Now I'm alone, and I don't know how to be alone. I'm too used to sharing everything with her, the girl I was never allowed to share anything with.

I grab my phone and look through it, trying to find something to occupy my time. After ordering a pizza, I look through my apps, hoping to find a game or something to play, but I find that dating app instead. A part of me thinks that she's probably deleted it by now, but another part wants to see if she'll talk to me, or Brandon, I guess. Since Maddie caught us, Jazz has been quiet, and that worries me. I'm sure she'd break up with me in a heartbeat if Maddie demanded it. But would she do that? Maddie loves both me and Jazz. She wants us happy, right? What if she's afraid to lose her best friend, a person that's always been by her side, to her big brother?

I quickly call Maddie, but she doesn't answer. She sends it directly to voicemail.

With nothing else to do while I wait for my pizza, I open the dating app.

Brandon: *How's it going? We haven't talked in a while.*

Jazz: *Not great. I'm sort of it a fight with my best friend, and now she won't answer my phone calls or texts.*

Brandon: *What was the fight about?*

Jazz: *That guy I told you about, I started seeing him. And it was great and magical. But he is her older brother, and I kept it from her. I've kept a lot of things from her over the years.*

Brandon: *Well, if she's as good of a friend as you say, she'll understand. Just give her some time.*

Jazz: *That's the same thing Damon said. But enough about me, how have you been? How's it going with that girl?*

Brandon: *LOL, amazing, actually. I think I'm in love.*

Jazz: *OMG, that's great!*

Brandon: *It is, but I'm afraid I'm going to lose her.*

Jazz: *Why? Did something happen?*

Brandon: *A long story that I don't want to get into right now. I didn't do anything wrong, but I'm starting to worry that our relationship is too hard on her. Like maybe this on top of everything else in life, work, friends, family, it's all too much. Make sense, or am I crazy?*

Jazz: *It makes sense. But I don't think you should assume it's too hard on her. Maybe she's stressed, but I'm sure if you and she are anything like Damon and me, coming home to you is what removes the stress. He's my home, and being with him is the only thing that matters. Are you two like that?*

I smile from hearing her describe our relationship.

Brandon: *I think we are.*

Jazz: *Don't give up hope. Everything works out in the end.*

Brandon: *Thanks for the kind words. I was really needing some positivity.*

Jazz: *Kind of crazy how we started out looking for a date on here and ended up as friends. I think we both knew our heart wasn't into dating someone else. I haven't told Damon about this app yet or our friendship. Think I should?*

Brandon: *Yeah, I agree. I hope you didn't feel I led you on at all? I certainly wanted to move on with someone else...or at least that's what I told myself. Is he the jealous type? LOL*

Jazz: *I don't know. Sort of, I guess. When it comes to me, anyway. He's protective. And no, I don't feel that way at all. I think we both wanted to find others even though our hearts weren't in it.*

Brandon: *I don't think you should keep any secrets. I mean, it's not like we're doing anything wrong. We're not trying to meet up or date. What problem could he have with it?*

Jazz: *Good point. I hate to rush away, but I'm missing my boyfriend right now. I think I'll call him.*

Brandon: *Okay, have a good night, and I hope you and your friend can make things right.*

Jazz: *Me too, and hang in there. Sometimes girls get a little overwhelmed with everything. When she has her head on right, she'll be back in your arms in no time.*

15

JAZMINE

I don't know why but talking with Brandon always puts things into perspective for me. And talking to him really makes me miss Damon and our nightly talks. I close out of the app and dial Damon's number. He answers on the third ring.

"Hey, beautiful. How's it going?" He sounds much more chipper than he did the last I saw him.

"Okay, I guess. I can't get Maddie to answer her phone." I pour a glass of wine and take a seat on the couch.

"I couldn't either. I tried calling her. She's probably with that new boyfriend of hers."

"I miss you," I confess.

"I miss you too," he breathes out.

"Come over?" I ask, shyly.

"Absolutely."

"And bring dinner?" I add on.

"Already ordered a pizza. Be there soon."

"Damon?"

"Yeah?"

"I love you."

I can hear his smile in his voice. "I love you, too."

Without another word, he hangs up the phone, and I pick up my glass of wine, finishing it off.

A few minutes later, someone is knocking on the door, and I run to answer it, thinking it's Damon. I pull it open quickly with a big smile on my face to find Maddie.

"Oh my God, Maddie. I've been calling you for hours. Where have you been?" I ask, pulling her against me for a hug.

"I just needed to take a walk and clear my head. I'm ready now."

I pull her into the house and lead her to the couch. Sitting at her side, I start. "We weren't trying to hide anything from you, Mads. The only reason we kept it a secret is because it was so new, we wanted to adjust to us being a couple before bringing anyone else in. And then we wanted to make sure it was going to last. We didn't want to involve the family, you know. We didn't know if you guys would be happy or upset. I mean, what Damon and I have going, it started when we were much younger. You know I've always been in love with him. And, as it turns out, he's always been in love with me. He was just too worried about our age difference growing up, and then we were both finally old enough, he was leaving for college. It's just a mess, but trust me, we weren't hiding it from you."

She nods her head. "I do understand, Jazz. I'm just worried, that's all. I've seen Damon move from girl to girl without a care in the world. I mean, last year, he brought home two different girls for Thanksgiving and Christmas. I don't want him to do that to you."

I take her hand in mine. "He won't."

"How do you know?" She cocks her head to the side.

"Trust. I know it's weird, but the way he is with me, it's completely different. With those other women, he was cold and careless. With me, he's warm and inviting. He's romantic. I mean, he took me back to your childhood house so we could rewrite our memories."

She nods. "I ran into Mrs. Weaver yesterday. She and my mom still talk. She brought up how wonderful it was to see you two together."

My mouth drops open. "She did?"

She nods. "Yep."

"Oh, my God. What did your mom say? Is she mad?"

"She insisted that it wasn't true. She said she would know if something like that was going on. That's why I barged into the office today. I had to find out, and I knew if you were together and you hadn't told me, you wouldn't come clean if I asked. I'm actually really happy that you're together. I'm happy you're finally happy, but I swear, if he treats you like one of those random girls, I'm going to kick his ass."

We both laugh, and I pull her in for another hug. "Let's never fight again."

"Deal," she agrees.

"And let's promise always to tell each other everything."

"Agreed."

We hear the front door open and we pull apart and turn in time to see Damon walk in with a pizza in hand. He sees the two of us and freezes.

"Everything okay with you two?"

I smile. "Perfect."

He nods. "Good. Mads, pizza?" He points to the box.

"Thanks, but I have a dinner date with Travis." She stands.

"Things are getting serious, huh?" I ask.

She shrugs. "Who knows? You'll find out when I do," she says stepping past Damon and out the door.

Damon places the box on the coffee table and sits next to me. I immediately move to straddle him. Wrapping my arms around his neck, I lean in for a kiss. His hands hold my hips firmly and he deepens the kiss.

"We were only apart a few hours and already I missed you like crazy."

"I missed you too. I went home and was lost without you there to talk to and cuddle with," he says with a grin. "God, I can't believe I sound like such a douche right now."

I laugh. "Well, we have another problem to solve."

"What's that?"

"Your MILF from the other day told your mom and Maddie that we're together."

"What?"

I nod. "Maddie said your mom insisted it wasn't true, that she'd know if something like that was going on."

He groans and lets his head fall back against the couch.

"Looks like we have to tell them this weekend. If we want this to work between us, we can't keep secrets with each other or with our family."

"Okay, this weekend," he agrees.

"I have one last thing to tell you."

"What?"

"Before we started doing what we're doing, I joined a dating app. I found this guy named Brandon. I was interested in dating him, but then we hooked up, and it never went any further with him. I never met him, but we did talk a lot. He turned into a really good friend."

"Okay," he says, kind of awkward like. "Should I be worried about this guy?"

"No," I say quickly, shaking my head. "I just wanted you to know in case it ever came up. We're friends that talked online. We never met. And since we've gotten together, we don't talk much now anyway."

He shrugs. "Okay. I don't see a problem with it. I have friends too, Jazz."

"Really?"

"Really. Now, let's eat because I'm starving." He gently smacks my ass.

I laugh and crawl off of him so he can open the pizza box. We cuddle up with one another and eat our semi-cold pizza. We watch TV and laugh and talk. Before I know it, the room is dark, and he's passed out cold. I smile and close up the pizza box. Looking at him while he sleeps seals my fate. I want to marry him. I want us to live together, grow our lives together, make babies together.

I pick up my phone and send a quick message.

Jazz: *He's it for me. Thank you for your friendship, but I'm deleting this app because I no longer need it. I've found the one.*

I press send and a second later, his phone on the coffee table chimes.

That's weird, I think, leaning forward and seeing the notification from the same app.

Private Message From: Jazmine

My mouth drops open as I look between him and the phone.

He's Brandon.

He's been lying to me. Why would he do that? Why would he join the same app and talk to me using a fake picture and fake name? And all of this after agreeing to be honest with one another, even after I told him about my friendship with Brandon just to keep him in the loop?

I stand and pace the floor, not knowing what to do. *I mean, is it that big of a deal? Is it something I should just forget about? Oh, God. What if he's been talking to other girls the whole time? This is exactly what Maddie has been warning me about. How could I be so stupid?*

I bend down and pick up his phone, meaning to look through the app to see who all he's talked to. I swipe the screen, and it opens.

"Jazz? What are you doing?" he asks, rubbing sleep from his eyes.

I sit down beside him, his phone still in my hands. "I... um. I sent a message to Brandon, telling him how happy I am with you and how I was going to delete the app and no longer be able to talk to him."

He nods at first, but then his eyes go wide.

"Imagine my surprise when your phone goes off seconds after sending it." I hand his phone over.

He takes it, looks at me, the phone, and back. "Jazz, look." He throws the phone down and stands to explain.

"It's not what you think."

"Oh, it's not? You didn't start a fake profile just to talk to me under someone else's name?"

"No, I did do that, but you don't understand."

"Explain it to me then. Please, enlighten me."

"After you started working with me, I knew I had to get you to let your guard down some way. I was afraid you hated me after all the tricks and gags I played on you. I just thought that you'd never be able to develop any feelings for me because when you looked at me, you saw who I was, not who I am. So I started this dating profile so you could get to know me, the real me. The me I am today. The man that loves you and always has."

I nod my head. "Okay. And why didn't you tell me that when we were talking about not keeping secrets from each other and our families?"

He shakes his head. "I don't know. I didn't want to fuck up what we had going. I thought that I could delete the app and you'd never know. I thought you'd do the same. I wasn't hiding anything," he swears.

"How many girls have you been talking to on there?"

"Just you, I swear. You can look if you want to." When I don't take the phone he's trying to hand me, he tosses it to the couch and falls to his knees in front of me. "I didn't need dating apps to find women, Jazz. You know this. I only got it for you. Please, you're blowing this way out of proportion."

I laugh and nod my head, refusing to make eye contact because I need a moment to think. To think over this in every possible way. I can't do that when he's here, in my face, talking to me and trying to explain.

He places his hands on my hips. "Jazmine," he says in his sure, strong voice.

Finally, I meet his gaze.

"You know me," he starts.

"That's my point! It wouldn't be totally surprising to find out you've been dating multiple women at once with your track record. Now, would it?"

He bites his lower lip as his eyes fall. "No, I guess it wouldn't. But honestly, I never thought you looked at me that way."

"What way?" I ask, feeling offended at him trying to turn this around on me.

"The way everyone else looks at me." He stands and starts pacing. "When they look at me," he motions toward the world. "They see a cocky guy that has money and a parade of women. But that's not me. I only want one woman. I've only ever wanted one woman. You. And when I realized that I'd never be able to have you, I tried to make up for that. But no other woman could compare to you. I've tried replacing you with more women than I can count, and each and every one failed. They're not you. They could never be you. They didn't make me feel the way I feel when I'm with you."

Tears fill my eyes. I'm confused, but I know one thing. He's not lying. I've seen him lie many times over the course of our life, and right now, he's being raw and honest. I can tell by the tone of voice he's using, the way he's holding himself, the way his eyes are stretched wide, but glossy, like he's about to cry.

I take a deep breath and close my eyes, thinking it over. "I know you're telling me the truth, Damon. But what I don't understand is why you couldn't tell me all of this before. I told you everything."

"I didn't tell you because I was afraid you'd act like this. What I did was dishonest. But I did it out of love."

I nod my head. "But if you were afraid to tell me something as small as this because you were worried about my reaction, what's going to make you tell me the bigger things in the future?"

He shakes his head and starts pacing again. "It seems like you're just wanting out of this. Like you're trying to find any excuse you can. You pushed me away earlier when Maddie flipped out, and now you're pushing me away again because of a little mistake." He stops and turns toward me. "I'm not letting you push me away again. You want to be mad at me for what I did, fine. But I'm not leaving. I'm going to stay here, and you can yell at me, hit me, whatever you need to do to get it out of your system, but I'm not walking away from this, and neither are you. We've wanted this for too long to let it go to hell over one little mistake." He reaches for my arm and pulls me up against him. His hands cup my cheeks, and he looks deeply into my eyes. "I love you, Jazmine. I love you, and I want to spend the rest of my life with you. And I'll prove that to you over and over for the rest of my life." His lips press against mine, and his tongue slides into my mouth. Suddenly, I can't even remember what we were fighting about.

He's right. I've wanted him since I was a kid, since before I even know what love was. My heart and soul attached to his long ago, and I've been walking around so long without them, I didn't know what it felt like to be whole. For the first time in my life, I know where I'm supposed to be, and who I'm supposed to be with. All I need is him. Every time in my life when I needed someone, he's been there. He's been there defending me, protecting me, loving me—even if it was in his own way. What more could I ask for?

I move my arms around his neck and jump up, wrapping my legs around his hips. He catches me in the same instant, never breaking the kiss. He rushes forward, pressing my back to the wall so his hands are free to pull away my top. His lips break free.

"Let me show you how much I love you, how much I've always loved you," he whispers, moving his lips down my jaw and to my throat.

"Mmmm," I mumble, enjoying the way he takes complete control of my body. His hand slides behind my back and unlatches my bra. It pops open and falls down my arms. With his hands on my hips, lifting me higher, his mouth descends lower, showering my breasts with hard kisses and tender nibbles.

I grab a fist full of his hair and yank his head back, so our eyes lock. "Take me to the bedroom, Damon," I demand.

He smirks. "I guess that means you forgive me?"

"It means I'm not ready to throw away something I've wanted my entire life over one silly mistake."

Without another word from either of us, he carries me to the bedroom where we crash onto the bed, completely wrapped up in one another in every way possible.

16

DAMON

"Are you sure this looks okay?" Jazz asks me as she looks herself over in the mirror.

I glance over at her while I'm sitting on the corner of the bed, pulling on my shoes. "You look great. Why are you so worried? We're just going to my parents' house."

"I know, but we're breaking the news to them tonight."

I laugh. "My parents have known you since you were five-years-old. You don't have to worry; they already like you." I stand and step up behind her, pulling her hair away from her neck so I can press a kiss to her soft skin.

"They like me as Maddie's best friend. I need them to like me as your girlfriend and maybe a daughter-in-law one day."

I take ahold of her wrist and spin her around, catching her and pulling her to my chest. "There's no maybe about it. I will marry you one day. And then, you will be mine to torture for the rest of my life." I grin, pulling her in for a kiss while grabbing a hand full of her ass.

She squeals and giggles, pushing me back. "Don't even start." She points her finger at me. "We can't be late."

I roll my eyes. "I'm always late."

"Not anymore, you're not." She picks up her purse and motions for me to get out the door.

We make the quick drive over to my parents' house and her mom's car is already in the drive. Since we grew up neighbors and being as close as we were, our parents are good friends. Her mom is always at our family dinners and holidays.

I pull the Jeep into the drive and shut off the engine. I unbuckle my seatbelt and look over at her. She has her bottom lip pulled into her mouth, gently biting the skin. I pick up her hand and steal her attention away from her thoughts.

"It will be great. You'll see." I offer her a grin in hopes of settling her nerves.

She takes a deep breath and nods. "Okay, let's do this."

I quickly jump out and rush around to open her door. She always refuses to wait, but I catch it as she swings it open. I hold out my hand, and she takes it as she climbs down. I wrap her arm around mine and lead her to the door.

We're a close family, not one of those types that have to knock at their own parents' house. I reach out and open the door, allowing her to walk in ahead of me. We walk through the foyer and through the dining room, into the kitchen where my mom and hers are moving about, getting things ready for dinner.

They both look up as we enter, and everything gets tossed aside so they can rush up to us and pull us in for a hug.

"I'm so glad you're here," my mom says, stepping back. "Your stubborn father is out on the back patio trying to grill the steaks. Please, go help him before the fire department is called."

I laugh and head out, pinching Jazz's ass on the way by. She jumps and cuts her eyes to me but doesn't say anything that will give away what I've done. I let myself out the glass doors and find dad standing in front of the grill.

"How's it going, Dad?" I ask, stepping up to his side.

His green eyes lock on mine, and he pulls me in for a hug, slapping me on the back as he does so. "It'd be a lot better if I could get this damn grill to light."

I laugh, but then bend down and turn on the gas.

He shakes his head with a smile, but says, "You've always been such a smartass."

I laugh and grab a beer out of the cooler. "Why don't you have a seat and enjoy a beer and I'll cook the steaks?"

He takes the beer. "Sounds like a hell of a plan."

I get busy cleaning off the grates on the grill.

"So, tell me, what's new?" he asks, taking off his kiss the chef apron and sitting down.

I shrug, not sure what to say. Jazz and I agreed to tell all our parents together. "Not much, I guess. I went back to the old house the other day... just to check it out."

"Oh, yeah? How's it holding up? These last few years, I've been paying someone to handle the upkeep."

I nod. "It looks great. I was wondering if you were planning on selling it." Using the tongs, I pick up a steak and place it on the grill.

He takes a sip of his beer, thinking it over. "Well, I guess we need to. I've just been hanging onto it for you or Maddie. Which ever one of you wanted to settle down and start a family first."

"That's kind of why I was asking."

His brows skyrocket. "Dear lord, you didn't knock up one of your flings, did you?"

I laugh. "No, I'm just starting to think about settling down and maybe starting a family. I'd love to raise my kids there. We had such a good childhood."

Dad stands and smacks me on the back. "You mean, you want to live there so your kids can be just as crazy as you two were? Having pool parties while you're away, stealing beer out of your fridge, and catching the back yard on fire when a bunch of drunken teenagers decide to set off fireworks?"

I laugh. "Yeah, I guess so."

His green eyes meet mine. "If you're serious, it's yours. You don't have to buy it."

"No, Dad. I want to buy it. You and Mom can take a cruise or something with the money, take a vacation."

He snorts. "If you think I can get your mom to miss her book club, garden club, and high tea, you're dumber than I thought you were." He takes another drink. "It's yours, son."

I pull him in for a hug. "Thanks, Dad. But what are you going to give Maddie?"

He waves his hand through the air. "I'll figure something out."

Within the hour, we're all sitting at the dining room table: Mom and Dad, Maddie, Jazz, her mom Stacy, and myself.

"This steak is cooked to perfection, Damon," Mom says, taking a bite of her steak.

"Thank you," I say, cutting into my own.

"So, Jazmine, what have you been up to lately?" my mom asks, glancing between the two of us.

Jazz wipes her mouth with her napkin. "Well, actually..." She glances up at me.

I take her hand in mine, and every eye is on us. "Jazz and I have been seeing one another for a little while now. So, yes, what Mrs. Weaver told you, Mom, is true. But honestly, we weren't trying to hide it from any of you. It's just that we didn't know how it would all play out, and we didn't want to put any strain on the family. Now that we've been together for a while, and we see how great things are going, we finally decided to bring you all in on our little secret."

Everyone is watching us with wide eyes.

"Well, it's about damn time," Dad says, picking up his beer and taking a swig.

My mom laughs. "I agree. We've only been watching you two flirt back and forth now for fifteen years. I'm happy for the both of you."

Jazz and I look over at her mom. "I think I won," she says, looking between my mom and dad now.

"What? Won what?" Jazz asks.

"We've known for years that you two were in love. We finally decided to take bets on how long it would take the two of you to realize it," she says with a smile.

Jazz and I look at one another, then back to the rest of the family.

"So, this whole time, you guys knew?" Jazz asks. "You knew when we were in high school, when we were dating everyone but each other?"

The three of them nod.

"I thought you guys would get together for sure after that night in the garage," my dad says.

We both look at one another again, completely confused about how he even knew about that.

"That was right around the time I noticed things were coming up missing in the garage: my beer, gasoline, spray paint. So I took the handheld camcorder and stuck it in the corner of the room before we left that night. The next morning, I had quite the surprise."

I shake my head in annoyance. "I can't believe you guys knew about all this shit, and you never said anything. Nobody was ever grounded; we never got any kind of speech, nothing. What kind of parents are you?" I ask in a joking manner.

"It's funny how you keep saying *we*," Mom says around a fit of laughter.

"I wasn't the only one there! Maddie and Jazz were doing the same shit."

"They were, but you were the one that started all those parties. Plus, after a while, it became a little game for your mom and me. We'd go out and guess what we'd be coming home to. We'd sit back and watch as you guys ran around frantically trying to cover up all the evidence." He laughs. "Like that time you guys had that costume party for Halloween." He laughs deeply, having to hold his belly. "We'd received several calls from the neighbors that night saying that there were half-naked teenagers running all over the property. When we came home the next morning, you all had on mismatched costumes, and I think you all had to leave the breakfast table at least once to throw up."

Jazz looks at me. "And that was the last time I drank keg beer."

Everyone around the table starts laughing.

"Weren't you worried we'd get into trouble though? Get hurt? Hell, you were never worried you'd become grandparents at an early age?"

My Best Friend's Brother | 131

"Son, your parents are two old hippies. We've done it all and had a blast. What kind of people would we be if we didn't let you do the same things? We didn't want to rob you of those experiences. And, if we'd been like all the other parents, you guys wouldn't have felt comfortable doing it at home. You would have been sneaking away like all the other kids at your parties. And who knew what could've happened. The best thing was having you at home, where you were safe. Plus, we knew how well you watched over these girls."

Jazz looks up at me, and I reach out, pulling her against my shoulder and giving her a hug. It's funny how all this time, we thought we were pulling something over on them, and it turns out, they were the ones pulling something over on us. That's what it means to be a parent. That's the kind of thing I hope to get right.

After everyone finishes eating, Dad pulls me aside. His green eyes are bloodshot from drinking, and he's wearing a big smile. "I saved something for you. I knew you'd want it one of these days," he says, pulling me into his office.

"What is it?" I ask, sliding my hands into my pockets.

He opens up the closet, steps inside, and starts digging around. In the corner of the closet, buried under a massive amount of junk, is an old shoe box. He walks out and hands it over.

I frown, looking at the box.

"Look inside when you get home. You'll understand."

I shrug. "Alright." I pull him in for a hug. "I guess we're going to get going then. Early day tomorrow," I say, turning and leaving the room.

———

"COME ON! OPEN IT!" Jazz says, jumping up and down on the bed from her seated position.

I laugh. "Alright, already." I place the box on the bed in front of us and open the lid. Inside, it looks to be a lot of worthless junk.

Jazz inhales loudly as she picks up a keychain. It has an ice cream cone dangling from it. "You remember this? I gave this to you when I was six!" Her brown eyes are wide with excitement.

I laugh. "I do remember that. I had it on the key that went to my bike lock. I remember noticing it was gone, but thought it was stupid and didn't bother looking for it. He must have found it and put it up."

We go through the box and find notes between the two of us. At one point, Jazz and I took turns taping notes to one another's doors. Well, she taped them to mine, and I taped them to Maddie's. They're not real notes though; they're nothing more than childish insults.

Damon stinks, Jazmine licks bunny poop, and Damon is a loser are the extent of notes.

We keep digging and find little things like ticket stubs, birthday invitations, and pictures of us from over the years. In the bottom of the box is a memory card. I pick it up. "What do you think on this?"

"Let's find out." She takes it from my hands, grabs her computer, and slides the card into it. A video pops up and starts playing. It's us in the garage that night. There I am, drunk and swaying back and forth. There's Jazz in her hot pink bikini. Watching this video makes me realize that that moment was, in fact, real and not a dream. And it also puts things into perspective. What I remember of that 'dream,' our moment in the garage was hot and really got me going. But watching it now, it's laughable. I can clearly see how nervous I was; my hands were shaking my voice was high pitched. I remember spinning her around and pressing her back to the fridge, but in this video, we nearly fall in doing so.

We both laugh at our inexperience. "I can't believe your dad kept this for us."

I nod my head. "It makes me wonder how hard our moms were laughing when he showed them."

Jazz closes the computer and sets it on the table while I put all the little moments of our lives back into the box.

"There's one thing I know for sure."

"Whats that?" I ask, turning back to face her.

"We've gotten a lot better at being together." Her lips find mine and she kisses me deeply. I pull her closer as I roll us over, taking my place on top, a place I've always wanted to be and a place I'll always yearn for.

EPILOGUE

THREE MONTHS LATER...

Someone knocks on the door, and I spin around in time to see Damon walking in.

"How do you like your new office?" he asks, pulling me against his chest as he presses a kiss to my lips.

"I love it, but the view isn't as good," I tell him.

He glances out the window. "It's the exact same view my office has."

I shake my head. "You're not sitting across from me in this office."

He grins and shakes his head, closing the space between us as his lips softly press to mine. The kiss lasts for a few moments before he pulls away and slips my hair behind my ear. "Are you ready for your surprise?"

I smile, nearly jumping up and down. "Yes, what is it?"

"If I told you, it wouldn't be a surprise, now would it?" He takes my hand and pulls me toward the door.

An hour later, we're pulling up at his old childhood home, basically at our old childhood home. I look over at him with confusion on my face. "What are we doing here? Did you think of another memory we need to rewrite?"

He smirks. "Something like that." He puts the Jeep in park and steps out. "Come on."

I climb out and jog around the Jeep to him. He takes my hand in his and pulls me toward the front door. He slides the key into the lock and lets us in. The moment we step in, he flips on the light, and the foyer lights up. The last time we were here, the house didn't have any power.

"Has someone bought the house?" I ask, a little sad. I know many people have lived here since we grew up and left, but I hate to think about it. This place is ours, it holds our memories, and I don't want anyone else making new memories here besides us. This is where we grew up, where we learned how to love, and how to be a friend.

"Someone has bought the house," he says, leading me up to his old bedroom.

"Who? Who bought the house and is okay with us coming in here?"

He turns around. "Me. I bought the house for us." He drops down onto his knee and pulls out a small blue box.

Immediately, my mouth drops open, and I cover it with my hand.

"Jazmine, it's taken us way too long to get here, or, I guess, to get back here. I thought it only makes sense to start making new memories where so many of our older memories took place. We grew up here, and I want our children growing up here. I've loved you my entire life, and I promise I will always do so. Will you please, please put me out of my misery and marry me? I can't wait another day to call you my wife."

"You can't marry Damon, Maddie. He's your brother!" I say, stomping my foot at her while trying to pull on the white dress we made out of a shower curtain.

"So? I want to get married too," she argues.

Damon sticks his head into her room. "What are you two fighting about now?" He leans against the door frame and rolls his eyes.

"Who gets to marry ," Maddie says, turning in his direction.

He laughs. "You're both crazy. I'd never marry either one of you!"

I slowly walk up to him. "But I'll make you mud pies any time you want." I offer up a small smile.

He purses his lips together and thinks it over. "Okay, I'll marry you on one condition."

"What?" I ask, all too willing to do anything he asks.

"You have to go steal me cookies any time I tell you to." He grins.

I roll my eyes. "Fine." I agree.

Tears swell in my eyes and fall over the rims. I'm breathless and can't speak. All I can do is nod my head.

He takes my left hand and slides the ring onto my finger, then stands and pulls me against him for a lip-crushing kiss. His hands cup my cheeks as he deepens the kiss and walks me backward. "I wish I would've brought some cookies," I say around laughter and tears.

He laughs. "There's some down in the Jeep. You can go steal me some later," he says, bringing his lips back to mine.

I'm surprised when the back of my legs touch a bed. I break away and look around the dark room. "I can't believe you did all of this," I whisper, still looking at the room that's exactly how I remember it, everything down to the posters on the walls.

"Shh," he whispers. "We don't want to get caught." He lays me down and covers his body with mine, and it feels like we never even left this house. It feels like we're back where it all began.

His hands are quick with removing our clothing, and it feels like it's only been seconds when he's sliding into me, right where he belongs. The way our bodies fit together, it's like we were made for one another. And now, I know how true that is. We were put together for a reason. My father dying is what caused my mom to move us here. Maybe Damon is a gift from my father, whom I never really knew. He knew I'd need a strong man in my life to protect me and love me, and he gave me Damon. Even when we were both too afraid to admit how we felt, he was always here, loving me in his own way, protecting me just like a brother would.

When he sucks my nipple into his mouth while thrusting upward, my release breaks and rains down over my whole body; it stops my breathing completely. My heart feels like it skips a beat. My toes go numb, and my muscles tighten around him. I'm lost in him.

Moments later, he lets out a deep moan, and his hips begin twitching as he spills himself inside of me. His head comes to rest on my chest, listening to my heart racing for him. He lets out a long breath and presses a soft kiss to the swell of my breast.

Then reality sets in, and he pulls himself away. "I'm sorry, I didn't hurt you, did I?" he asks, moving to my side.

I shake my head. "No, we're fine."

With my words, he lays down beside me and pulls me to his chest. His hand lands gently on my stomach. "I can't wait to raise this little baby with you."

I let out a breath that sounds like a hum. "I can't either. You're going to be such a good daddy." I place my hand on his jaw and look into his green eyes.

He kisses me on the forehead. "And you're going to be a great mommy."

"Which room is going to be the nursery?"

He shrugs. "I guess it depends on if there's more than one in there. What do you say we sit back and watch history repeat itself?"

I smile just thinking about how wonderful it would be to watch our son and the neighbor girl next door spend their childhood falling in love.

"She'll be one lucky girl."

He laughs. "I think our son will be the lucky one."

As we lay in bed, remembering our past and dreaming about our future, I can't say I regret anything. Damon has said before that he regrets playing all those pranks on me as a kid, but I can't regret a second of it because all of that led us to where we are today. Sure, there were days when I thought we'd never happen, that us being together was just a beautiful dream. But now I know that us being together is a dream come true, and a dream that only gets better as time goes on. We had a wonderful childhood together, and we've only grown from there. Our friendship grew into love, and our love grew to create a family. A family of our very own that we get to create new memories with. It's funny how a single house can hold everything that makes you who you are. But that's exactly what this house does for us. If these walls could talk, it'd be able to share our whole lives, past, present, and future.

All of it centering around each other.

***

If you loved *My Best Friend's Brother* then don't miss out on *Billionaire With Benefits*

Turns out Mr. Sex-on-a-stick at my gym,
that I may or may not have blatantly ogled, while shamelessly flirting,
Is not only my new boss...
He's my brother's best friend.

GRAB Billionaire with Benefits HERE

BILLIONAIRE WITH BENEFITS
SNEAK PEEK

Turns out Mr. Sex-on-a-stick at my gym,
The one who overheard me describing the naughty things I'd do
to him,
Is not only my new boss...
He's my brother's best friend.

He's 6'4" of solid muscle,
With a mouth that could make a sailor blush,
And determined to make my toes curl.

In my defense, I tried to walk away.
But the moment I tasted his lips,
And felt his hard, chiseled body pressed against mine,
My panties melted and my resolve went out the window.

We laid out the ground rules:
1. No feelings
2. No commitments
3. Nobody finds out

It was all just delicious, secret fun,
Until it wasn't.
What's worse, knowing he's risking everything to be with you?
Or realizing your only option is to break your heart and walk away?

I can't let him throw his life away for me.
After all, we never promised each other forever.

PROLOGUE
MADDIE

I stir awake as the sheet drags across my bare skin. I blink against the sun that's streaming in through the cracked curtain and sigh as the feel of a large, warm hand travels up my thigh.

"Good morning, beautiful," he murmurs against my throat, followed by a soft nibble.

A shiver runs through my body as his tongue dances softly against my neck. I groan softly as my back arches off the bed, needing more from him. He senses my anticipation as he trails his fingertips from my knee up my inner thigh, dancing briefly across my clit, causing my hips to jut up further.

"Mmmm, does my naughty girl like that?" He teases me again, letting his fingertips stay a little longer this time, dragging them across my clit a few more times ever so lightly.

"I want—" the words trail off as my eyes close, and he sucks my earlobe into his mouth. His breath comes out in soft, warm puffs against my cheek as his finger slips between my folds.

"What do you want? I want to hear the words." I reach my hand down to force his fingers harder against me, but he grabs my wrist before I can make contact.

"Tsk, tsk" he clicks while fastening both of my wrists above my head. He places his hand beneath my chin and forces me to look at him in the eyes.

"What do you want, Madeline? I told you I want to hear it. Whatever you need or desire." The last part is a whisper as he leans down and plants a soft kiss on each of my very pert nipples. I groan as he bites them after the kiss.

"I need to cum—I want...I want you to make me cum." The words tumble from my mouth in a rush as he smiles against my breast.

"How?" My mind is a blur; I feel like I'm about to burst.

"Your tongue, hands. Lick me." The words continue to come out in a staccato pattern. Finally, he releases my hands as he moves down my body to settle between my thighs. He inhales as he runs his nose up my center before flicking his tongue across my clit. I can't contain the loud moan that escapes my throat as I fist the sheets in my hands.

He grips my thighs with each hand, his fingertips digging into my flesh as he devours me with voracity. His slow licks transform into deliberate flicks of his tongue peppered between deep passionate kisses against my most sensitive and intimate parts.

No man has ever made my body feel this way. No man has ever had this kind of power and control over my body, causing it to explode with ecstasy over and over. Even when my brain is telling me I can't possibly handle more, my body betrays me and surrenders to his every desire.

I can't hold back my climax any longer. Sweat beads on my forehead as my body stiffens and arches. Hips bucking against his face as he crooks his finger, I explode in pleasure. My vision blurs as the orgasm tears through my body, leaving me in a satisfied, limp puddle of limbs on the bed.

He crawls up my body and settles between my thighs, pressing his lips against mine as his tongue explores my own. I can taste my release on his mouth as his rigid cock presses at my opening, and my thighs fall open to welcome him.

His eyes lock on mine as his hips begin a rocking motion. He intertwines his fingers with my own, once again pinning them to the bed and using the leverage to thrust himself into me even further.

The moment is deep and intimate. Emotions swirl through my head as I try to drown them out and live in the moment. This thing between us started as purely physical; we promised each other no labels and no commitments. I thought I knew what I wanted. I thought I could keep feelings out of it, but now, I can only hope to survive the fallout when he walks away.

CHAPTER 1

MADDIE

"Pick up the phone," I say as the line rings for what has to be the twentieth time.

"Hello?" Jazz, my best friend—fiancée to my brother and expectant mother of his baby— answers around a giggle.

"Finally! What the hell were you doing?" I ask, clearly annoyed.

"Nothing. What's up?"

"I'm getting ready for my first boxing class, and you said weeks ago you'd go with me."

"To be fair, that was before I found out I was pregnant. Damon doesn't think it's a smart decision."

"Ugh, what does my stupid brother know? Plus, it's not like we're going to actually be fighting. We'll hit the bag a few times. And it wouldn't have killed you to let me know before right now."

"I'm sorry, Mads, but I don't think so." I can hear the uneasiness in her voice.

"Come on, Jazz. Please come with me. Just this once, or until I meet some people and get comfortable."

"I don't know. I mean, Damon and I kind of had plans for tonight."

I hear her softly giggle and whisper, "Quit it, I'm on the phone."

"Seriously? You had plans with ME first! Jazz, did you forget you're my best friend first and his fiancée second? Since you guys have been hooking up, we don't ever see one another anymore. Come on. It's only for one hour, and then you can go home and do whatever you guys do with your nights." I silently gag at the end of that sentence.

"Okay, okay. You're right. I'm sorry." She lets out a sigh of defeat. "I'll be over in an hour."

"Thank you," I say, hanging up the phone. I hate having to play the *you were my best friend before his fiancée* card, but hey, a girl's gotta do what a girl's gotta do.

I drop the phone onto the couch and get up to change my clothes. I pull on a pair of black leggings and yank off my shirt to replace it with a lime-green sports bra. I check myself over in the mirror as I pull my hair up into a messy ponytail, then slide on my shoes. I do a few chores around the house, and just as I'm grabbing my jacket, phone, and keys, Jazz is walking in the door.

She lets out a deep breath and drops her purse on the table. "This is going to be a lot harder once Damon and I move out of the city, you know?"

I nod my head. "I know. All those nights we snuck out of the 'burbs to come to the city, and now you're moving back there voluntarily."

She offers a sad smile. "I know. But it's perfect if you think about it. I mean, how many people get to raise their kids in the same place they grew up? And with their childhood crush, no less?"

"It is kind of perfect." I stick my tongue out at her for having such a fairytale life.

She laughs. "I don't know what you expect me to do at this boxing class in my current condition." She motions toward her stomach that's still flat.

"You can do anything I'm going to do. It's the first class, so it's not like we're going to be fighting one another."

"Good, because I promised Damon that I wouldn't even put on gloves." She laughs.

"He thinks you're going to a boxing class to not box?" I ask, pulling my jacket on.

"He thinks I'm going for moral support."

"Why does he think that?" I ask, holding the door open to let her walk out first so I can lock it behind us.

"Because that's what I told him?"

We both laugh as we walk down the hall toward the main exit.

Twenty minutes later, we're at the gym, boxing gloves in place. I promise Jazz I won't tell my brother. The big room has punching bags hanging from the rafters and a ring in the far corner. The instructor tells us to warm up by jumping rope and trying out the bags. At first, we take turns holding the bag for our partner to hit. After a good twenty minutes of this, the instructor gets our attention again and has us sit down to watch two trained members fight as he walks us through what they're doing and why they're doing it.

Jazz and I sit ringside on the floor. The instructor is a middle-aged man with cropped graying hair and arms like pythons. A large vein runs down the center of his bicep. If I had to guess, I'd say he's the owner, and these are the fighters he's trained. Two more men join him in the ring.

I bump Jazz's elbow with mine. "Whoa! That guy is sexy as FUCK," I whisper so only she hears.

She nods her head and purses her lips together. "I guess. He's got nothing on Damon though."

I scoff and roll my eyes. "You two make me sick," I say, watching the man that's caught my eye.

He has dark hair that's shaved short, nearly to his scalp, and five o'clock shadow that does little to mask his chiseled jawline. Every time he jabs, his entire body flexes, and let me tell you, there's not an ounce of fat on his delicious physique. Every single muscle looks hard as a rock, like he's been hand carved out of granite by the gods. His chin is defined, with a small dimple in the center.

Suddenly, his emerald green eyes cut to me, and I feel like a kid with her hand caught in the cookie jar. He gives me a quick smirk, and I lick my lips as I feel my face grow red before looking away.

They fight for several minutes, and if you ask me, it isn't nearly long enough. Then, the three men move out of the ring and onto the floor.

"All of you, go back to your bags and use the information we just gave you to improve. I want to see you strict on form. Plant that back leg and lean into the punches you throw. We'll all be walking around the room, giving you pointers," the older man says.

Jazz and I stand up and move back to our punching bag. She holds the bag and I step in front of it. Curling my hands into tight fists inside my gloves, I hit the bag over and over. I actually forget where I am, paying no mind to the people around me or the sexy man that could be watching me. I'm focusing all my energy on that bag and the power behind my punch.

"You have pretty good form. Is this your first time?" the sexy guy asks, stepping next to Jazz, facing me.

I let my arms fall to my sides as I nod my head, unable to speak. I don't know if it's because I'm breathless from the relentless punching or if it's because I'm at a loss for words given how much sexier he is up close.

He has his arms crossed over his sculpted chest, causing his biceps to bulge as he looks me up and down. "Can I give you some pointers?"

"Of course," I agree, trying to sound nonchalant. In reality, I'm about to melt into a puddle on the spot.

"Take your position," he orders.

I bring my fists back up.

He walks a circle around me.

"Spread your feet," he says, gently pushing them further apart with his foot.

I do as he says.

"Straighten your back." He places one hand flat on my spine, causing me to suck in a breath from the electric current that cuts through me. He steps to my side and places the other hand on my stomach. "Tighten your abs. Can you feel that? The difference in how you were standing and how you're standing now. You're taller, tighter.

All your muscles are under your control. Keep that core engaged; don't let your spine hunch."

I nod, now focusing more on how his hands are touching me rather than listening to what he's saying.

"Now, jab!"

I extend my arm and hit the bag. It makes a thumping sound that fills my ears.

"Good. Keep your wrist straight," he tells me. "Again!"

I extend my arm again, this time focusing on keeping my wrist straight. The blow is much more solid than the previous ones.

"Better. Now, when you swing, put your whole body into it. Again!"

I swing with all my might while keeping my wrist straight. The strike is solid and powerful.

"There," he says, letting his hands drop. "Much better."

"Thanks," I say a little too breathy for my liking.

He looks at Jazz. "You need some tips?"

She shakes her head. "Nope. I'm only here for support."

He lets out a deep chuckle. "Alright." He looks back at me, but he doesn't just look at me: his eyes roam up me until they meet mine, like a lion staring at an antelope he's about to devour. "Keep going. I'll check back with you later." Without another word, he walks away to help the next person.

For the rest of the class, I watch him out of the corner of my eye, checking to see if he helps another person the way he helped me. He doesn't touch them at all. The most he does is walk by with a nod, sometimes offering a quick comment. I'm not sure if I should be creeped out by that knowledge or accept that maybe my form was just that shitty.

When the class is dismissed, Jazz and I stand at the counter, removing our gloves.

"Hey, what happened to the guy you were dating? Travis?" Jazz asks, arching an eyebrow.

I roll my eyes. "Travis was fun." I shrug. "He was like a toy, but you know, all toys get old after a while. So, I donated him for the next girl to enjoy." I smile.

Jazz shakes her head. "One of these days, the love bug will bite you."

I laugh. "I don't know about the love bug, but I'd definitely take a hit from that sexy boxer."

"Is that right?" he asks, stepping up behind me.

My face immediately heats up and I bite my lower lip as I turn around to face him. *Shit!*

He offers me a grin as his eyes travel up my body again. "I'm here most nights. If you want a private lesson, you know where to find me." He shoots me a wink and walks away.

When he's far enough away from me, a long breath I didn't realize I was holding escapes my mouth and my shoulders fall.

"Really? You couldn't tell me he was behind me? Mouth, meet foot."

Jazz laughs. "I thought it'd be funnier this way. Not to mention, now you have a reason to come back."

I grab my jacket and pull it on. "I already had a reason to come back; now I have a reason to completely avoid this place."

"What? Why would you do that? I thought you wanted to take a hit from that boxer?" she teases.

I bump her arm with my elbow. "Because I'm completely embarrassed!"

"Oh, you'll be fine. I've seen you recover from much worse. But on another note, I'm meeting up with Damon for dinner. Want to join? We're going to your favorite pizza place."

"I don't want to be your third wheel," I complain.

She opens the door and walks out onto the sidewalk. "Seriously, it's always been the three of us. Nothing changed, Mads."

"Nothing changed? Jazz you're carrying his baby and you guys are in a relationship. Now you have all the little inside jokes and communicate with stupid looks like you and I always did." I know I'm sulking, but I'm still not over the moon that I was pushed out of the group. "Whatever, I'll go. But I'm ordering my own breadsticks."

She laughs. "Deal."

Jazz and I walk into the pizza place a little while later and Damon is already at a table waiting. When he sees us, he stands and pulls Jazz in for a hug and a quick kiss. I slide into the booth and pick up a menu.

"How was the class?" he asks.

"Well, your sister got hit on by a hot boxer," Jazz says, wrapping her hands around Damon's arm.

"That's gross," Damon mumbles, picking up his water and taking a sip.

"I didn't get hit on. I got invited to a private lesson." I smile, just hearing myself saying the words.

"That's worse. Who is this guy?" Damon looks between the two of us, brows pulled together and eyes bouncing from her to me.

"I didn't catch his name, but he has sweaty muscles for days, dark hair, a face I could mount, and bright green eyes. Like, his eyes were green-green. Not your dull, boring green."

Damon holds up his hands and waves them back and forth violently. "I NEVER want to hear those words again, Maddie. Jesus!"

"I think your eyes are gorgeous, babe," Jazz says, squeezing his arm.

Damon smirks as he turns to admire her.

When they start kissing, I can't help but roll my eyes and sigh loudly. I'm still not over the disgust of watching my brother suck my best friend's face.

"We seriously need to find Maddie someone to settle down with," Jazz says, running the tips of her fingers up and down Damon's forearm.

"You guys are killing me. I mean, can't we just have dinner like we used to? You know, you two throwing insults at one another, making me laugh? Now it's like a god damn porno every time we hang out."

"Oh, I have my first doctor's appointment tomorrow. We get to find out how far along I am and see our little baby," she gushes, ignoring my comments.

"I thought you were six weeks along?" I ask.

"Well, that's what I'm guessing, but I have no real way of knowing because we were just doing it all the time," she laughs. This is usually the talk I like, but knowing my brother is involved makes me want to barf.

"Ew, all right. I've had enough. I'm going to grab a hot and ready pizza on my way home. You two, enjoy your night," I say, scooting out of the bench.

"No, Mads, please stay. We don't hang out much anymore," Jazz says, trying to stand up to stop me, but she's on the inside of the booth and Damon isn't moving.

"You know, I'm really tired, and I'm just going to crash. But thanks for the invite and for going with me." I'm already walking backward toward the door, so they can't stop me.

The moment I step out into the cool night air, I feel like I can finally breathe. I suck in a big breath, hold it a second, and let it all out. I can feel the annoyance and stress leave my body at the same time. I hope Jazz and Damon don't think that I'm not happy for them, because I am. I'm celebrating that they got together, but I'm also mourning the loss of my best friend. She's no longer just my best friend; now she's his fiancée, and soon, she'll be a mom.

Jazz just got her dream job too. Her life is going places, and I'm still stuck in the mailroom, waiting for my desired position to open up. When I started a year ago, I was told it would only be a couple of weeks before I could move into data configuration, but here I am, still stuck sorting mail.

I don't have my dream job. I don't have a special person to share things with. I'm not about to have a baby—thank god. And, I no longer have a best friend that's always down to hang out. What do I have?

I have a large pizza to myself. I smile as I look down at the warm box and take in a big whiff of the gooey cheese.

When I get home, I kick off my shoes but don't bother to change. I drop all my takeout on the coffee table and flip on the tv. I flop onto the couch and pull the blanket around myself. As I search for something to watch, I move all the food up onto the sofa, so I don't have to reach for it. I look around my lonely, quiet apartment and wish I had someone to share this with. I never understood why people got into serious relationships until I saw Jazz and Damon. They're literally never alone. They work together and then come home to each other. They always have someone to talk to, someone to eat with, and someone to hold them when they feel lonely. Maybe I should put myself out there and make it clear I want a relationship instead of random hookups and flings.

I shake my head. What the fuck am I thinking? I like being single. I like getting dressed up and looking hot. I like the chase. I like a no-strings-attached fling. I like having complete control over the TV, and I like for things to be where I left them. I'm obviously way too tired if I'm even considering giving all this up.

I push all thoughts away as I dig into my food and watch reality TV all alone, with nobody to complain.

GRAB Billionaire with Benefits HERE

READ THE REST OF THE MAKE HER MINE SERIES

Billionaire With Benefits
My Boss's Sister
My Best Friend's Ex
Best Friend's Baby

ALSO BY ALEXIS WINTER

Men of Rocky Mountain Series

Claiming Her Forever

A Second Chance at Forever

Love You Forever Series

The Wrong Brother

Marrying My Best Friend's BFF

Breaking Up with My Boss

My Accidental Forever

The F It List

The Baby Fling

Grand Lake Colorado Series

A Complete Small-Town Contemporary Romance Collection

Slade Brothers Series

Billionaire's Unexpected Bride

Off Limits Daddy

Baby Secret

Loves me NOT

Best Friend's Sister

Castille Hotel Series

Hate That I Love You

Business & Pleasure

Baby Mistake

Fake It

Mountain Ridge Series

Just Friends: Mountain Ridge Book 1

Protect Me: Mountain Ridge Book 2

Baby Shock: Mountain Ridge Book 3

South Side Boys Series

Bad Boy Protector-Book 1

Fake Boyfriend-Book 2

Brother-in-law's Baby-Book 3

Bad Boy's Baby-Book 4

ALL BOOKS CAN BE READ AS STAND-ALONE READS WITHIN THESE SERIES

ABOUT THE AUTHOR

Alexis Winter is a contemporary romance author who loves to share her steamy stories with the world. She specializes in billionaires, alpha males and the women they love.

If you love to curl up with a good romance book you will certainly enjoy her work. Whether it's a story about an innocent young woman learning about the world or a sassy and fierce heroine who knows what she wants you,'re sure to enjoy the happily ever afters she provides.

When Alexis isn't writing away furiously, you can find her exploring the Rocky Mountains, traveling, enjoying a glass of wine or petting a cat.

You can find her books on Amazon or here: https://www.alexiswinterauthor.com/